A Beautiful
Catastrophe

A Beautiful Catastrophe

Aut viam inveniam aut faciam

Nikita Achanta

PARTRIDGE

A Penguin Random House Company

To order additional copies of this book, contact
Partridge India
000 800 10062 62
orders.india@partridgepublishing.com

www.partridgepublishing.com/india

<u>about the author.</u>

"You are so busy being you that you have no idea how utterly unprecedented you are," John Green.

A wise man once said, "The only way to deal with an unfree world is to become so absolutely free that your very existence is an act of rebellion," and that's what Nikita believes in.

The name's Nikita Achanta, 17 and she studies at the Mayo College Girls' School, Ajmer. Her interests range from reading novels and comics, especially Garfield, to listening to music, playing the guitar, video games, and writing. She writes a lot, from quotes to articles to poems. She has an undying love for dogs, resulting in her persuasion to adopt a dog when she was seven years old. And, call it fate, her parents gifted her a Golden Retriever for her 17th birthday [The 6th of October], and life has been happier ever since.

She wrote this book after her 10th grade board exams, during the three-month break. She was 16 years old then.

A little more information?

Things she likes:

Band/Artist(s) – Pink Floyd, Oasis, The Beatles, Dire Straits, Poets of the Fall, Green Day, Linkin Park, Imagine Dragons, Foo Fighters, Katy Perry, Paramore, Porcupine Tree, Iron Maiden, Disturbed.

Athlete(s) – Lionel Messi and David Villa.

Football Club and Country – FC Barcelona, Argentina National Football Team, Selección de fútbol de España (Spain National Football Team).

Subject(s) – Psychology, English.

Colour(s) – Black, Blue, Green.

Video Games(s) – Assassin's Creed series, FIFA 14, Star Wars: The Force Unleashed II, The Final Fantasy Series, Halo Series, Need for Speed: Hot Pursuit, Tomb Raider.

Celebrity(s) – Johnny Depp, Cillian Murphy, James Spader, William Shatner, Tom Hiddleston, Jim Parsons, Gary Oldman, Alan Rickman, Tom Felton, Tom Cruise, Ben Whishaw, Benedict Cumberbatch, Nathan Fillion, Martin Freeman, Andrew Scott, Rupert Graves, Robert Downey Jr., Heath Ledger, Jude Law, Stana Katic, Liv Tyler, Sofia Vergara, Angelina Jolie, Julia Roberts, Candice Bergen, Sushmita Sen.

<u>TV show(s)</u> – Sherlock, House MD, Modern Family, Boston Legal, Supernatural, Merlin, Doctor Who, Castle, The Blacklist, Peaky Binders, The Way We Live Now, The Big Bang Theory, Koffee with Karan, Comedy Nights with Kapil, Man vs. Wild, Untamed and Uncut, South Park, Whose Line Is It Anyway?

<u>Book(s)</u> – Harry Potter series, The Hunger Games trilogy, Garfield Comics, Tintin series, Asterix series, Percy Jackson series, Divergent trilogy, Achieve Your Highest Potential: Be The Best You Can Be, Artemis Fowl series, The Inheritance Cycle, Heat Wave, Naked Heat, Heat Rises, Moby Dick, Life of Pi, Perks of Being a Wallflower, To Kill A Mockingbird, Illusions, Jonathan Livingston Seagull, Will Grayson Will Grayson, Paper Towns, Let It Snow, The Fault in our Stars, John Dies at the End, The Five People You Meet in Heaven, Sherlock Holmes.

<u>Author(s)</u> – Chitra Jha, JK Rowling, Suzanne Collins, Christopher Paolini, Herge, Jim Davis, Eoin Colfer, Richard Bach, Jeffery Archer, John Green, Veronica Ruth, Sir Arthur Conan Doyle.

<u>Superhero(s)</u> – Iron Man, Batman, Wolverine.

<u>Super-villain(s)</u> – Loki, Magneto, The Joker, The Scarecrow, Darth Vader, Jim Moriarty.

<u>Twitter</u> – @NikitaAchanta.

foreword.

It's just a silly foreword. Get over it.

Note: <u>All characters appearing in this work are fictitious… well… never mind. Any resemblance to real persons, living or dead, is purely coincidental. Err… not really… but… erm… forget about that</u>.

preface.

This book started off as a journal. I thought I could keep a journal, like all of us do. But I couldn't. Gradually, it came out to be a novel. I started writing this book as soon as my 10th class Board exams came to an end, and believe it or not, I finished writing this book in less than a week. I used to write day and night because words were flowing out like endless rain into a paper cup, to quote The Beatles. I did have a phase of writer's block towards the end of the book. I sat on my laptop and opened up the document but I didn't know what to write. I froze. But I still finished the book within the first week of my three-month holiday period.

I hope you enjoy the book. Live long and prosper.

<u>acknowledgement.</u>

Thanks, ma and dad, for the gift of life.
My brother, Nikhil Achanta, who is simply the most amazing and inspirational person I know. His everlasting support and never-ending knowledge inspired me to become a better person.

People say that you shouldn't speak to strangers on the internet, but thank god I did. I would like to express my gratitude to my two crazy best friends, Manisha Singh and Dimple Anand. Thanks a ton for making me cry and then making me laugh. No one could have given me better advice than these two lunatics.

The dedication of my life is split seven ways.

To **Severus Snape**, for teaching me that love is the strongest force in this world and for teaching me how to be brave and stand up to the world's expectations.

To **Sherlock Holmes**, who taught me to have faith, stand strong in the face of denial and ridicule, and above all, believe. Also, biscuits cure all.

To **Loki Laufeyson**, who taught me that we don't always have to fall, we can choose to jump.

To **Sam and Dean Winchester**, who taught me that when everything fails, there's family. That no matter what, your brother's going to be there for you. Always.

To **Dr. Jonathan Crane**, for proving and sealing it that one's life is governed by fear and that fear will slowly swallow you whole if you don't fight back.

To **Timekeeper Raymond Leon**, who taught me that time is power and that it'll slowly take you away if you don't utilise it properly. We didn't start the clock, and we surely can't stop it. Every second counts.

To **Artemis Fowl**, who taught me that the coldest hearts are often the loneliest. It takes somebody open enough to warm them up.

characteristic description.

<u>Nikita Achanta aka Nixter</u> - "My thoughts are stars I cannot fathom into constellations."

That's me, yes. I'm just your irregular, immature, self centred, ignorant, I-am-a-professional-at-pushing-people-away kind of person. That's one way to put it. I'm about 5'7". I have brownish black hair which reaches the length of not more than my neck. I have eyes of the same colour which peer through a pair of spectacles. Basically tomboyish. My main interests are music, gadgets and books. I love rock and heavy metal, making Disturbed, Porcupine Tree, Poets of the Fall and Green Day my favourite bands, or for soft music, basically Oasis, Pink Floyd and The Beatles. I am also prone to falling in love with celebrities who don't even know I exist. I support FC Barcelona, Argentina National Football Club and Selección de fútbol de España. I love reading novels. They are my escape from this godforsaken world. Also, I will judge you by your music taste and whether you read books or not. I like muffins, books, chocolates, ice-cream, pizza, pasta and coffee.

<u>Ashwini Kamboj aka Ash</u> – "Grief does not change you; it reveals you."

She's barely 5'6''. I I believe she's a little off her brain, but that's just what I think. And that, I believe, is the truth. With long jet black hair and icy cold black eyes, Ashwini is quite street smart. She doesn't like my music interests which make us quite opposite. She's very much into Hindi music and movies but I don't like music and movies in that language much. Ashwini is my companion in all my adventures. She thinks I'm a lunatic at times because I fall in love with fictional characters and celebrities. Ashwini likes... err... I don't even know, man. She's my best friend and I don't even know. Sad, isn't it? She just doesn't speak of her obsessions like I do. She's not a fangirl like I am. She didn't get sucked into the fandom life. Also, she likes to think of me as the reserved types, one who doesn't speak her mind openly. Well then.

<u>Mini ma'am</u> – "I'm actually walking around in a bit of a haze after I finish reading a book – spellbound and looking at everything through a different prism."

An amazing personality with an amazing control over the language of English, Mini ma'am is one of the five English teachers in our school and my favourite. With dark brown medium length hair and brownish eyes, she wears reading glasses whenever she's teaching, or needs to see far, which I confirmed later. The two of us have a little in common - our unconditional love for books, Tom Cruise and Julia Roberts. She likes books, coffee and me! Okay, I'll shut up.

<u>Naaz Kapoor</u> – "The marks humans leave are too often scars."

Naaz is a year junior to me. About 5'5" with long jet black hair, Naaz is one person I can talk to about the most random of things. By the way, I pull her legs a lot and tease her like anything.

<u>Dhruv and Lakshita Jain aka Dex and Lex</u> – "You die in the middle of your life, in the middle of a sentence."

Siblings, and two of the craziest and most insane people I've ever met. Lakshita is this girl with amazing brown hair which she ties into a pony. She's short, which means she's closer to hell. Just kidding. And Dhruv? That guy's mental. In a good way. A guy obsessed with The Hunger Games and madly in love with Katie Holmes. The two of us together are insane. As he says, he's on a rollercoaster that only goes up, quoting John Green. He also used to have this little puppy crush on me. He's into quoting John Green every now and then because he has this crazy obsession with his writings. Dhruv is the guy with black messed up hair, jet black eyes, his face sunk in showing his sharp cheekbones. I usually refer to him as 'jackass' because he and I share a love-hate relationship. Dhruv is the guy with the amazing drumming skills and Lakshita is the girl with the... err... well... she doesn't have musical intelligence, but yes, she sure is my fangirl-mate and one who shares obsessions similar to mine.

‼

There are some things one should know before reading this book.

ob·ses·sion /əbˈseSHən/
    The state of being obsessed with someone or something. An idea or thought that continually preoccupies or intrudes on a person's mind.

cock·y /ˈkäkē/
    Conceited or arrogant, esp. in a bold or cheeky way.

com·pe·tent /ˈkämpətənt/
    Having the necessary ability, knowledge, or skill to do something successfully. Efficient and capable.

cyn·i·cal /ˈsinikəl/
    Believing that people are motivated by self-interest; distrustful of human sincerity or integrity. Doubtful as to whether something will happen or is worthwhile.

ma·lev·o·lent /mə'levələnt/

Showing a desire to resist authority, control, or convention.

an·ti·so·cial /ˌantē'sōSHəl/

Contrary to the laws and customs of society; devoid of or antagonistic to sociable instincts or practices. Not sociable; not wanting the company of others.

mis·an·thrope /'misən,THrōp/

A person who dislikes humankind and avoids human society.

sin·is·ter /'sinistər/

Giving the impression that something harmful or evil is happening or will happen. Wicked or criminal.

sar·cas·tic /sär'kastik/

Marked by or given to using irony in order to mock or convey contempt

book·worm /'book,wərm/

A person devoted to reading. The larva of a wood-boring beetle that feeds on the paper and glue in books.

fangirl

A rabid breed of human female who is obsessed with either a fictional character or an actor.

My name is Nikita Achanta, and this is my story.

part one.

one.

I wrote frantically, trying not to mess up the calculation. It was a little hard completing the last sum with my teacher staring at me as I wrote. I looked up at her once as she stood there, tapping her feet and waiting for me to be done with my exam.

"Hurry up, Nikita," she said.

I sighed as I tried to multiply 18 by 8. I shook my head once. She sighed much more heavily and said, "It's just a math exam, and the room is empty because everyone's done with their paper and left. You might want to hurry up." I nodded once and glanced at the question paper one last time. I wrote the concluding line and heard Shruti ma'am yell, "Oh, just put the pen down!" I put the pen down immediately and brought my hands to my shoulder, speaking defensively, "It's a pen, woman, not an AK-47." She leaned forward to take my paper and spoke close to my face in her cold voice, more like whispered, "If you weren't my favourite student, I would have sent you out of the class long ago." I pulled up my smug grin and said, my voice low and cold, "Why, aren't you adorable." She rolled her eyes as she arranged my answer sheet in the pile, looking at the thick pile. She looked at me as I put my pen and geometric instruments in my kit, and then asked, "How many extra sheets did you use, Nikita?" I zipped the kit and stretched my arms and back. I then clacked my finger together, hoping that they hadn't gone all numb. I put both my hands around my neck and clacked my neck once. I then looked at her and said, "Ten, or eleven. What does it matter?" She chuckled and asked straightforwardly, "You'll pass?" I got up from my seat as she completed that question. I gasped a little, and then ran my left hand through my hair. I chuckled and replied, looking around, "These are boards. It's not pre-boards that I won't cross the 50-mark. Don't worry. I'll pass, with a good grade too. You won't see me in 10th again." She smiled at me as I picked up my bag and shoved my kit in, hanging my bag on one shoulder. I was about to walk out of the class. I turned around and saw her arranging all the answer sheets according to the students' roll numbers.

[Author's note! Quick description of Shruti ma'am. That's my second favourite teacher, yes. I could talk to her about novels all day long. She teaches English at school. She teases and taunts as well. Especially me. It's like I'm her main target or something. She pulls my legs anytime an opportunity flashes by.]

She felt my presence and looked at me as she arranged the answer sheets. "Yes, Nikita?" she asked, looking down at the thick pile.

"Thank you," I said, my lips curved up into the usual smirk. "For everything."

She looked at me and I looked at her. She smiled and replied, "You're a brilliant kid, and I'm proud of you."

I smiled and nodded my head as I turned around and walked out of the room. I looked around the floor corridor and sighed. I blinked once and then said to myself, "And to think I'm done with this place forever now." I shook my head and walked downstairs, sliding over the stairs' railing. I jumped off the railing and walked out of the school building.

I looked to my left and I saw Ashwini standing there, moving her hands in all directions, yelling at Dhruv. I rolled my eyes and shoved my hands into my jacket's pockets and walked up to them.

"You should have known better! Why didn't you tell me I was solving the sum wrong?" Ashwini yelled at Dhruv, who seemed pretty helpless. He shook his head and yelled back in his husky voice, "I was sitting seven seats away from you! How do you expect a guy, sitting seven seats away, to tell you how to solve a math question?" Ashwini clenched her fist and was almost about to punch Dhruv in the face. I gritted my teeth together and hurriedly went and stood between the two. I grabbed Ashwini's fist as soon as she lifted it to my face level.

"Don't punch him. That pretty face is the only asset he has," I said seriously.

Ashwini pulled her fist back and folded her arms, looking away. I sighed as I saw that anger in her eyes. I shook my head and turned to Dhruv. He looked at me and smiled – his usual crooked smile which any girl would go head over heels for – except for me, so says Ashwini.

I sighed again and asked, "Why must you provoke her time and again?" He raised his eyebrows and spoke defensively, "I just... I don't... whose... whose side are you... are you even on?" I folded my arms and replied blandly, "Probably Lakshita's because she's not here." I wriggled my eyebrows and looked around. I looked at Ashwini and questioned, "Where is Lex?" Ashwini was bursting in flames. She answered as she looked away, "I don't know." I bit my lower lip as I heard her say that, and soon as I turned around, Lakshita came hopping from the school building. I peeked over Dhruv's shoulder and then whispered to him, "She looks utterly happy. That intrigues me." Dhruv chuckled and turned around, looking at his sister, practically dancing with every hop she took. She came and stood in front of us, with a broad smile on her face.

I questioned out of surprise, "You look very happy. You do realise that disgusts me?" She nodded her head but didn't speak a word. I continued, titling my head to one side, "But since you've lost your voice temporarily, you don't disgust me that much." She pouted and looked down. I laughed and looked over at Ashwini, who was still angry. I walked up to Ashwini and grabbed her by her shoulders and shook her. She looked at me with a disgusted look. I said in an excited tone, "Come on. You promised you'd take me for a ride on your scooty after our exams were over. And look! They're over now!" She smirked without saying a word. I got closer to her and whispered in my cold tone, "Take. Me. For.

A. Ride." She looked at me sheepishly and nodded her head, "Fine." I grinned broadly and she led the way, bumping Dhruv out of her way and not looking at him once. I followed her, and stopped for a moment in front of Dhruv. I whispered, "Be careful, Dex. You don't want to mess around with her." He nodded his head out of disagreement, smirked a little and whispered, "You'll save me from her though, that I am sure of." I looked at him, his face close to mine. I chuckled and replied, "Why not, jackass?" I punched his shoulder and as I did, Ashwini yelled, "Nikita Achanta, do you want to come or should I take my unicorn and fly away!?" I was taken aback a little by her words, because I remembered her saying last summer that she had no interest in unicorns. I stuck my tongue out at Dhruv and ran over to rejoin Ashwini.

"You give the poor boy a hard time," I said to her.

She kept on looking forward as we walked. She then shook her head and said, "He really likes you, you know that, right?" She smiled a little, looking at me as I cleared my throat, ignored the comment and put my arm around her shoulder and spoke to her in a low voice, "Look, Ash, I realise you had a bad exam, but don't take your anger out on me." She looked down as the two of us walked and replied in the same pitch, "I was caught a little off guard by the question paper. It was so trifling!" I rolled my eyes and said, "You're telling me." She continued, "And plus..." Before she could finish the sentence, two kids ran over and bumped into her, running ahead of us. She yelled in anger, "Mind your manners!" She shook her fist and sighed. I smirked unpleasantly and said, "Peasants." Ashwini gave me a gesture of disgust and said helplessly, "Nikita, please don't use such words. Bad language doesn't suit you." I shrugged my shoulders and replied, "Fine then. Filty mudbloods. And they're foul, loathsome, evil little cockroaches." Ashwini sighed heavily and said, raising her voice a little, "Will you please stop making Harry Potter references during every little conversation we have!?" I tilted my head to one side, folded my arms and said, "If I could, I would, but since I can't, I shan't." Ashwini put her hand to her forehead, and made choking motions with the other, saying, "And stop quoting The Big Bang Theory." I rolled my eyes in disapproval. I looked at her and said, "You were saying something about the examination." She looked at me with a look of remembrance and said, "Oh yeah! And plus, Mini ma'am had her adjustment in our class…"

Again, before she could complete her sentence, my eyes grew wide and my jaw dropped, I interrupted in between and said, "Oh."

She looked at me with a look of pettiness and asked, "What?" I ran both my hands through my hair and answered, "Ashwini, go home." She looked at me, raising one eyebrow, and questioned again, "Home? But you wanted a ride and…" I interrupted once again and answered, tapping my feet impatiently, "How about you change your clothes and meet me at my place in about an hour? Sound good?" She was about to say something, but before she could, I smiled and said, "Wonderful! See you then!"

I put my feet to the test and ran towards the school building, not looking back at Ashwini, but I looked at her once as she said with disgust, "And the attention span of a squirrel!"

two.

I ran frantically towards the building, gently pushing the other students out of the way, saying, "Excuse me! Sorry! Coming through!"

I entered the building and one of my seniors who I despised, Sneha, stood there, admiring herself in the reflection of the notice board's glass. She turned around and saw me, and I saw her smile fade away. I casually walked past her but was stopped as she shouted from behind, "Wait!"

I sighed in frustration, turned around and looked at her in utter disgust. She walked up to me with her huge belly and her floppy hair. She flicked her hair to one side and said to me, "The whole school's empty. All your friends have gone home. What business do you have?" I glanced at her and spoke in my confident oratory voice, "Last time I checked, you did not run this school. People more capable, than you, do." Her face turned into one of an uglier toad than it already was. She let out a lot of air from her nostrils, and then replied in disgust, "So you're an admin of five pages on Facebook. You have a twitter account with a pretty good follow count, and you have a roleplaying Twitter account too. What the hell are you doing with your life?" I chuckled and spoke in my previous tone, with wriggling eyebrows, "Probably something that you'll never be able to achieve. Something you can't even imagine to be a part of. Okay, bye."

With those words, I turned my back to her as I saw her jaw drop, and I made my way up the stairs. As I walked up the stairs, I said to myself, "See? This is why you should never mess with an orator." I chuckled at my own statement and rushed up the stairs.

I covered one floor, sighed a little and then made my way up to the second floor. I grabbed the greasy railing and walked up the stairs. I reached the second floor and stood in between the two divisions of the hallway. I looked around, and made my way to the left one, because my instincts tingled. I walked slowly, peeking into every classroom as I moved across. I crossed one classroom and then stopped. I walked backwards and peeked into the classroom once again. Mini ma'am sat on one of the tables near the window, sunlight falling on her long brown hair. She adjusted her glasses once and used her red Parker to correct the answer sheets. I smiled a little, and was about to enter the room, but stopped. I took a step back and knocked at the open door. Mini ma'am looked up and saw me, the girl with the messy short hair and spectacles around her eyes.

A broad smile covered her lips and she said, "And all this time I was thinking where you were."

I shifted my eyes slightly and then replied, "I do have the attention span of a squirrel." She chuckled and said, "Come on in, Nikita." I smiled and walked in and made my way up to her. She put her pen down and looked up at me. She then asked, "Have a seat?" I shook my head and answered, "I'm good, thanks." She then asked, "What brings you here?" I leaned against the table and folded my arms. I looked up at the ceiling and replied, "Well, mainly because you'd kill me if I hadn't come to see you." Her jaw dropped and she asked, once again, in her sarcastic voice, "So that's the reputation I have? Very well, Nixter." I laughed lightly and looked down at her. I stuck my tongue out at her and saw a grin cover her lips. She picked up her pen, uncapped it and starting correcting the answer sheets again.

I said in a serious tone, "I was kidding. I came to see you to say goodbye." I bit my lower lip and looked out of the window, with my eyebrows crossed. She dropped her pen while writing and looked at me with the same seriousness. She then chuckled and said, "You do know how to make a good joke." I shifted my gaze to her and replied, "I'm not joking." She pushed back into her chair, putting one arm of hers on the chair's sidearm. She said with a little seriousness, "You can't leave. You have three months of holidays if you don't plan to stay in this school." I raised my shoulders a little and then dropped them. I moved my tongue around my mouth, and then pressed it to one side of my left cheek. I scratched the back of my head and replied, "Three months till I leave for Mayo."

She smiled a little and said, "Bigger avenues."

I nodded. She got up from her chair, putting the pile of answer sheets down on her chair. Our gaze met and she said in a low pitch, "I still have your coffee to be tasted." I moved my hands a little and slipped them into my jacket's pockets, and said, "Yes. But I make hot chocolate even better." She rolled her eyes, put her left hand on my right shoulder and replied, "That's good. I'll take that as an invitation." I smiled and looked at her, leaning forward a little, I said, "Beware I have a dog." She pouted. I retracted back to my leaning position and said with a little smirk, "Don't worry. I don't set him on people I care about." She smiled and put her hand back. She sighed and reached her right hand forward. I looked at her hand and then back at her. She said, "I'll see you then." I reached for her hand as I replied, "You will." As I took her hand, she pulled me in for a hug, and hugged me tightly. I buried my head in her shoulder as she said, "Till next time, take care, kiddo." I nodded once and hugged her back tightly. I pulled away after a few seconds and passed her a smile.

She sighed happily and said, "Somehow your cynical way of talking and that cold, calm voice of yours, really gets to me." I looked at her and replied, "Well, we have two years of obsession with Cillian Murphy to thank for that." She chuckled and said, "Guy's hot." I replied in my cold and calm voice, "Can't say I haven't taught you anything. I'll catch you later." She nodded once with a smile on her face. As I was about to walk out, she stopped me, calling from behind, "Nikita?" I looked at her, with my hands shoved in my pockets, and asked, "Yes?" She walked a little closer to me and said, "Uh, Sarah's having her birthday party, so she asked me to invite you, and your group: Ashwini,

Lakshita, Dhruv and Naaz." I raised my eyebrows and burst out laughing. I then said, after stopping my laughter, "Why on earth would your daughter, Sarah, invite me to her birthday party?" Mini ma'am folded her arms and lightly crossed her eyebrows, not getting much of what I was saying. I scratched my cheek and continued, "Your daughter despises me, if you haven't already noticed it." Mini ma'am sighed and replied, "She doesn't despise you. Yes, she, being a 13-year old, doesn't like a few of your habits, but she doesn't despise you completely." I nodded my head in amusement, chuckled and said, "You're charming, you know that? Alright then. Her birthday's on the 6th of April, next month, right?" She nodded her head once and I said, "I'll make it. I'll make sure my group makes it too." She smiled, clapping her hands happily, and said, "Brilliant!" I raised my eyebrows again and asked, "But it's just the 14th of March today. Isn't it a little early to hand out the invitations?" She pulled my cheek a little roughly this time and answered, "My twisted daughter thinks that you might come up with some or the other plan, to blow up the world or something." She let go off my cheek. I rubbed my cheek gently and said, "Great, I'll put my plans of world domination at a hold, then." She laughed and I laughed along. I flicked my hair to one side and said, pointing my clenched fist with my thumb in an upright position, to the door, "I should really go now." She nodded her head one last time. She raised her fist and said, "Fist-bump?" I smiled and bumped my fist lightly against hers. I took my fist back and said, looking her straight in the eyes, "One last time: I still owe you a coffee. My place, anytime." She smiled and replied, "I'll keep that in mind."

I took a bow and walked out of the room as she smiled at me one last time.

three.

I opened the door and walked inside my house. The house smelt of the flowers, rajnigandha. I sniffed the air and looked around. I walked in further and saw three of our servants cleaning up the house. I had never seen the house being cleaned so vigorously. I looked towards the kitchen and mum stood there, with a cooking apron on, as she moved the spatula around in a frying pan. She stood there with her back turned towards me, engrossed in cooking as she read the instructions to the recipe from her green Sony laptop. I walked up to the kitchen and leaned against the wall.

I folded my arms and said, "Wow, mother. I walked into the house and no one got to know a thing." She jumped into the air a little with the astonishment. She turned towards me, still moving the spatula with her hand. I smirked as she said, "Oh, for goodness sake, this is what happens when you play Assassin's Creed a lot." I chuckled and replied, "You should be happy that I do something productive and worthwhile, unlike my other friends, who spend their time talking about boys and TV shows." She looked at the frying pan, added some oil to it and moved the spatula around and said, moving her hand in the air to clear off the smoke, "I'll give you that one, Nikita." I smiled and said, "See? It's why I hate those muggles." My mum looked at me and said bluntly, "Cute, very cute." I nodded my head. She put down the spatula and reached out to open one of the cabinets to get a packet of peanuts. She then asked, "Things apart: How was your exam?" I pretended to shift my eyes around and then answered, letting a sigh out of my mouth, "It was good. I'll pass the 70-mark." She looked at me with her eyes wide and asked again, "That good?" I nodded my head quickly. She opened the packet of peanuts and put them in the frying pan. I walked up to the stove and looked into the frying pan. "Hmm, that's peanuts, tons of dark chocolate, milk and butter. Buttermilk too," I thought to myself. I got excited as I thought, "Oh God, she's making me a dessert!" I looked happily at my mum, who was now taking out some more pans. I asked happily, "Ma, you making me a dessert? Has anyone ever told you that you're the most brilliant mother ever? I love you for this." She walked up to the stove and put a deeper frying pan, lighting up the stove, and said plainly, "It's not for you, Nikita." My happiness dropped and I asked, "For whom, then?" She put some butter into the other frying pan and said, "Your father invited Kapil uncle and Sherry aunty over for dinner." I widened my eyes and asked, "Tonight!?" She looked at me and nodded. I put both my hands on her shoulders, turning her towards me, and questioned me, "Mum! Where's my approval to this?" She looked at me with a deranged look, folded her arms and said, "Your approval?" I shrugged my shoulders and said, "Yes! They have an 11-year old daughter. You know how much I disapprove of kids anywhere in my vicinity." She rolled her eyes and replied, "Bear with me, Nikita. Besides, you rarely come out of your room." I looked at her, my jaw dropped, and said, "See? This is one of the reasons we should be glad that we're rich and I have my own room. You're right. I'm just going to lock myself in there for tonight."

She nodded once and got back to her cooking after saying, "Good. Now, go away, and let me cook." I let out some air from my nostrils and said, "You know, sometimes being 'Forever Alone' sucks, Ma." She looked at me and replied, sympathetically, "It's okay, kiddo. Happens." I sighed heavily and turned around to go upstairs to my room. I walked up the stairs, sliding my hand along with the wooden railing and went to my room. I opened the door and turned on the lights. I was taken aback a little because my room was a mess. I sighed happily and said to myself, "At least there's one thing that's as messy as me. Hello, room."

I walked in and shut the door behind me. I chucked my bag on the beanbag, slipping off my shoes; I fell straight on the bed like a dead man. I buried my face in my pillow and sighed deeply. I then looked to my side table and picked up my iPhone which lay on my copy of Illusions by Richard Bach.

I rolled over, my face to the ceiling, and scrolled through my messages, thinking, "Hmm... 8 Twitter notifications... wait. Why is this Belieber following me? No! Anyway, ah, 3 new texts and 2 missed calls. Don't the people who call realise I'll be at school? I sometimes doubt there's any hope for humanity." I put my iPhone back on my book and covered my face with both my hands. I sighed once again, content with the feeling that I was finally done with Sant Nischal Singh Public School. I was content with the feeling that I wouldn't have to cope up with everyone's shit every other day – that I wouldn't have to spend six hours with people who didn't care about me; that I wouldn't have to cope with the peer pressure; that I wouldn't have to cope up with the math syllabus. I was happy. But somewhere inside, I was a little upset, thinking I was going to leave this place forever. I was going to meet new people. Thousands of thoughts galloped inside my head: Will my new classmates like me? Will I like them? Will they be Potterheads? Or people who like South Park and who obsess over fictional characters and celebrities? Will they understand me? Will they share my music interests? So many questions to which I had no answers. I turned over to my other side, removing my glasses and closed my eyes. "For in dreams, we enter a world that's entirely our own," as Albus Dumbledore would say. And before I knew it, I was sound asleep, and I couldn't help but think, "My life would make a pretty decent book."

I opened my eyes, feeling the presence of something staring at my face. I rolled over and gently opened my eyes. My eyes widened as I saw Ashwini sitting next to me and staring at my face. I immediately got up and sat on my bed, astonishingly saying, "What the hell are you doing here?!" She coughed a little and replied, "You said that we were going to take a ride on my activa. You seem to have forgotten." I sighed deeply, blinked once and said in a sleepy voice, "Yeah,

I... um... must have dozed off." She stood up, nodding once and stretched her hands. I looked at her and asked, my eyebrows lightly crossed, "How... How long have you been here?" She clacked her neck sideways and replied in a sheepish voice, "An hour, I guess." I was shocked by that answer, rubbing my hands together, I asked again, "And what were you doing for the past hour I was asleep?" She walked up to my bookcase, rubbing her chin, she answered, "Going through your book collection." She kneeled down, running her hands over my Harry Potter series. I looked over to her and said disgustingly, "You hate books." She nodded her head once and replied, going through the books, "Can't say I don't. But I'm thinking of reading Harry Potter, since your praise it so much." I smiled happily, got up from my bed and slipped my feet into my slippers. I walked up to her, hands shoved in my pockets, and said happily, "That's great, Ash! Can't say I haven't taught you a thing or two either." I kneeled down next to her, picking up my copy of Harry Potter and the Deathly Hallows, I held it close to me and continued, "And if you need anything, being the huge Potterhead that I am, please, don't hesitate to ask." She looked at me and said with a shine in her eyes, "That's awesome! Can I borrow your Harry Potter books then?" She reached her hand forward for my Deathly Hallows copy, the one which I held close to me. I pulled back, hugging my book and replied with a little seriousness, "Except that. No one takes my Harry Potter books." She pouted, with her eyebrows crossed and stood up. I put my copy of

Deathly Hallows back, patted it one last time, and stood up. Ashwini rubbed both her temples.

I looked at her and asked, "All okay?" She nodded once, with her eyes shut, fingers still on her temples. I sighed, then chuckled, and said, "Forget about that. You have plans tonight?" She opened her eyes and nodded quickly. I sighed deeply and asked again, "Plans? It's holidays! What plans do you have now?" She shoved both her hands in her jeans' pockets and replied, "I have to study for this entrance exam I'm appearing for." I frowned and said in an angry tone, "Ashwini..." She looked away, with a slight smirk on her lips, and folded arms. I put both my hands on her shoulders and turned her towards me with a jerk. She widened her eyes as her body jerked towards me. I looked into her eyes and spoke in my cold voice, near her face, "Look, we just finished with exams. I know, getting entrance in +1 in another school is something the two of us have to work on. But don't just get started all of a sudden!" She shrugged her shoulders and interrupted, saying, "Nikita, it's..." I put my finger on her lips, stopping her from continuing. I adjusted my glasses with one hand while the other still rested on Ashwini's shoulder, and continued, "Yes, yes, it's important. It's important for me, too. But have you forgotten? To not to forget to take a breath." She looked down, with crossed eyebrows, an expression of hers I had gotten used to. I lifted her face by her chin and saw her eyes fill with tears. My eyes widened at the sight and I asked, slapping her cheek lightly, "Dude, what happened?" She shook her head, biting her lower lip, and said, "I just... I had a really bad math exam... I don't even know if they'll take me in at DPS..." My eyes filled with a little sympathy and I said to her, "Look, we all have bad exams. But mark my words; you're going to get it. You never fail at math. NEVER. So don't, even for once, think that you're not going to get through, okay?" She sniffed once, wiping away a tear streaming down her cheek with her left palm. I slapped her cheek lightly again and said, "Hey, hey, hey, why are you even worrying about the future? Don't you remember that chapter in our Hindi book? It said that grieving over the past and worrying about the future, will not bring you anything at all." She looked up at me, sniffed once, and nodded her head slightly. I continued, maintaining the same cold voice, "So stop grieving and worrying and live in today. Carpe diem! Seize the day, Ashwini. Because the present is the only truth. Nothing else. Yesterday is a lie and tomorrow is an undefined truth. So yeah." She sniffed again, letting out a short sigh.

I ran my hand through her hair, ruffling it a bit, and continued, "So, carpe diem, dude." I smiled as I finished my sentence.

Ashwini looked up at the ceiling, pulling back her tears, and then looked at me, with a little smile on her face. I put both my hands down and shoved them in my school uniform's jacket's pockets. She asked with a smile, "How come you're not a counsellor?" I shrugged my shoulders lightly, answering, "Well, I try my best." She chuckled and I smiled. I pulled one of my hands out of my pockets and pulled one of her cheeks lightly. I smiled and said, "See? You look better this way." I pulled my hand back and she rubbed her cheek. She chuckled and replied, "Wow, Nikita. You've grown a heart." I raised an eyebrow in astonishment, moving my hands completely against her words, I protested, "No, no, no. I am a heartless creature. Learn to live with that." She quivered her lips and said, tauntingly, "Dr. Jonathan Crane has taught you stuff, hasn't he?" I nodded once and replied, not noticing her taunt, "Every super villain has. Loki, Crowley, Scarecrow, Joker, Moriarty, Darth Vader, you know." She nodded her head helplessly and said, "You know; normal people are inspired by superheroes. They usually hate super villains. I hate super villains. They're so evil!" I curled my fingers together like an Italian and said, "It's why they're called super 'villains'. And I beg to differ! Without super villains, and without my Scarecrow, your Batman would be out of job. Think about that!" I folded my arms confidently. Ashwini struggled for words. She filled her mouth with air and let it out slowly, saying, "I can't argue with the district's number one orator, now can I?" I shook my head with pleasure, a grin covering my lips. She chuckled, running a hand through her jet black hair, and said, "So I'll cancel my plans for tonight." I smiled and excitedly clapped my hands, hopping into the air. She looked at me with a deranged look and asked, "Um, why are you so happy?" I stopped clapping and hopping, and spoke with a pleasant smile, "Because you, my best friend, and I are going to spend tonight, at your place, watching some or the other movie." She widened her eyes and asked, "Wait! Um… why?" I joined my hands together and said, with puppy eyes, "Please?" She looked at me and asked, yet again, "You do realise that you and I share no alike interests when it comes to movies and music, right? I can't stand one night with you watching English movies, Nikita. Just no." She walked up to my study table and started reading some of my poems pasted on the cabinets. I stood behind her and said helplessly, "Alright, fine! We'll watch some Hindi movies then." She turned towards me and asked, "You'll survive?" I nodded my head, pouting my lips a bit. She sighed and said, "How about we kick off with 127 Hours, and the Rush Hour Trilogy, maybe?" I looked up at her with my eyes lit up and I said, "That's insane! I mean, that sounds awesome! Here's what I'm thinking. Let's watch Red Eye tonight." Ashwini sighed and said, "Just because the love of your life is in it? No, thanks."

"It's a brilliant movie!"

"Really now?"

"It is."

"I know it is. But —"

"And because Cilly's in it. I always wanted to be Rachel McAdams in Red Eye. Not because she's gorgeous, but because Cillian is."

"Then you'd have to stab him in the throat," Ashwini said, folding her arms cockily.

"No, no, no, I won't do that. I'd make a plot-twist."

"Do tell."

"Kiss him during the lavatory scene. Think about that possibility."

"Kissing him would be nice."

"What?"

"I mean… yeah, for you!"

"Hmm. His lips sure look delicious."

"Nikita, stop."

"Right. Apologies. But can you just…" I sighed dreamily.

"Okay, now what?"

"Jackson Rippner. Hotness written all over."

"He was a cold assassin!"

"I loved Cilly in Red Eye. He seemed like a badass, cold-hearted assassin, but that character had so many depths. He's incredibly sexy."

"Tell me something new, will you?"

"Oo."

"Now what?"

"Jackson Rippner can lock me in an airplane bathroom with him anytime."

She chuckled slightly and smiled at me and asked, "Riddle me this." I bit my lower lip and replied, "Shoot." She continued with her question, "Why this sudden movie marathon thing? We never do that." I shifted my eyes, trying to make up reasons and excuses. I struggled for words and said, slipping my hands into my lower's pockets, "Well, I just thought it would help us bond." I nodded my head once and continued, "You know, improve our friendship." I almost made that sound like a question, like I was unsure. Ashwini grinned, folding her arms and asked, "Gotcha. Whom are you avoiding tonight?" My smirk faded and I stumbled for words, but replied, "No one! I just want to spend time with you." She narrowed her eyes, looking me straight in the eye. I sighed deeply and confessed, "Fine! There are people coming over for dinner and…" Before I could complete my sentence, Ashwini said, folding her arms, "...And anti-social Nikita is showing." I nodded my head, pouting my lips. She shook her head, chuckling and replied, "Fine, we'll have a movie night tonight then." My eyes lit up and Ashwini smiled. She was about to say something, but her phone rang. She took it out of her pocket, looking at the screen, her eyes widened and she gestured a minute to me. She picked up her phone and spoke into it, "Yeah, mum?" She turned her back towards me. I took my iPhone out of my pocket and started fiddling with it. I heard Ashwini speak into the phone, one hand to her ear and the other on the back of her head, "But mum... Nikita... I... yes, mum. I'll do that. Okay, mum. Bye, mum. I love you too, mum." She hung up and shoved the phone in her pocket angrily. I looked up at her as she turned around to face me. I saw an unpleasant smirk cover her lips. Out of question, I asked, "All okay?" She shook her head and said in a low pitch, "I'm sorry, Achanta. No movie night tonight." My jaw dropped and happiness went out and sadness set in. I asked her, my vocalization almost a yell, "But why!? You just said... that we'd... I was... Rush Hour... Ashwini!"

"Look, I'm sorry. I wanted to do this more than you, you realize that?"

"Then why cancel it?"

"Because mum has guests coming over... And—"

"And as usual, Miss Ashwini has to be Miss Social, right?"

"Nikita..."

"Get out of my sight before I pick up a knife and hold it to your throat."

She stomped her foot hard on the ground, flicked her hair and walked out of my room, shutting the door behind her. I clenched my fists and tugged at my hair in anger.

four.

"Mum?" I peeked into her room; she sat on her bed, putting on some earrings.

She asked with her back towards me, "Yes?" I walked into her room and said nervously, "Er... You know Sarah?" She turned around to look at me, and then replied, "Mini ma'am's daughter, who doesn't know her? One brilliant child." I smirked unpleasant, almost speaking to myself, "Wouldn't kill to call me 'brilliant', for once." She looked at me, lightly crossing her eyebrows, and asked, "What's that?" My eyes widened a little and I replied, out of the blue, "Huh? Nothing. Nope." Mum smirked and asked, yet again, "So, what about Sarah?" I shoved my hands into my jean's pockets and replied in the same nervous tone, "She's having her birthday party on the 6th... and she invited me. So... can I go? Please?" Mum looked up at me and nodded once with a quiet smile on her face. I smiled a little and bowed. I turned around and walked out of her room and into the lobby. I turned on the main TV system, and then turned on the Xbox and 48' LED screen. I picked up the Assassin's Creed III disc and put it in the console.

I picked up the wireless controller and fell lifelessly on the couch. I yawned and scrolled through the main menu of my Xbox 360, signed into my profile titled "Nixter" and clicked on the Assassin's Creed III icon. I started playing the game, being a professional video-gamer that I was, chopping of heads, stabbing Red Coats in the chest, jumping into haystacks, robbing people, acting all cool and shit. A cut-scene triggered. I sighed, pulled up my left arm's sleeve and looked at my WE watch, which had London's flag designed around the strap. It was 8:30 pm. I smirked and looked back at the screen, and as I did, the bell rang. I shouted, my eyes fixed on the screen, "Ma! Someone's at the door!" Not even a moment passed, mum walked out of her room and headed for the door. She stopped and whispered from behind the couch, "Kid, please do not cringe." I shook my head and replied in my cold voice, "I do not intend to cringe. People make me cringe. Especially muggles." She rolled her eyes and opened the door. I leaned back, turned my head towards the door and saw the guests arriving. I yawned again, my eyes almost closing. I blinked twice, trying to keep my eyes open. I looked at the screen once, deciding to ignore the lot till they actually reached the lobby. I skipped the cut-scene and entered a fight with some Red Coats. My brain thought of nothing else but the screen.

"Grab."

"Now counter."

"Flip him over."

"Tomahawk in the throat, blade in the chest."

"Back flip."

"Stab. Jump."

"Brace."

"Punch. Slash."

"Block."

"Now kill."

I smiled widely as I rotated the joystick to look at the battalion I eliminated. "Thirty one... thirty two... three... four... five... six... seven... eight... nine... and... Forty-one down! Hell yes!" I almost shouted in pleasure.

"Forty-one, wow." I turned my head around, a little taken aback by the voice. I smiled as I saw Kapil uncle standing there. I chuckled, putting my controller on the couch, and said, "Yeah, I've done better." He laughed. I stood up and shook his hand firmly, smiling, "Good to see you, sir." He smiled, shaking my hand, and replied, "Great to see you. Been too long." I took back my hand and shoved them in my jeans' pockets. I shrugged and said, "I had exams. You know... tenth grade sucks." He nodded and smiled a little, "School life's the best, though." I smirked and replied, "I'll pretend I did not hear that." He laughed. I turned off the console, putting the controller back in its place, and turned off the main TV system. I walked around the couch and met Sherry aunty and her daughter, Aishwarya, as well.

An hour or two passed.

Mum, dad, I and their family sat in the drawing room. Drinks, snacks, talks, laughs.

"So, Nikita," Kapil uncle asked as I took a sip of my coke. I looked at him and asked, "Sir?" He questioned, "You like video games?" I smiled and thought to myself, "Finally a topic I can relate to." I nodded once

and answered, "Yes, I'm a professional video-gamer."
He asked once again, tossing a nutcracker into his
mouth, "What genres?" I cackled my fingers together
and replied, "RPG, sport, action-adventure. Mostly
games which involve me killing people. I like blood."
He nodded his head a little. His daughter, Aishwarya,
asked in between, "That game you were playing...
killing people..." I looked at her, sitting across the room
on the couch, and said in my cold voice, "Assassin's
Creed III. I don't like it when people don't remember
video-game names." Her shoulders drooped a little; she
continued with her question, "Yes, yes, I've heard of
the game. What's that guy's name, again?" I clenched
my right fist which lay inside my pocket. I replied
with a pleasant smile, trying not to look disappointed,
"Ratonhnhaké:ton." She raised both her eyebrows in
astonishment of the sound of the name. "Err..." She
said. "I'm not even going to try to pronounce that." I
smirked unpleasantly.

Later...

We were done with dinner and were sitting in the
garden. Mum and Sherry aunty sat on the swing,
while dad and Kapil uncle sat on the black metallic
chairs, Aishwarya sat on a small chair and I sat on
the ground. Everyone was just talking, and I was just
sitting there, trying to keep my eyes open. I yawned
once, bringing my knees to my chin, resting my chin
on my knees, I wrapped my arms around my knees.
Aishwarya looked at me and asked, "Why sit on the

ground? It's cold." I raised my eyes to look up at her. I sighed and replied, "It makes me feel close to nature." She laughed out loud. "Seriously?" She asked. I shifted my eyes to my mum, who was smiling on hearing me say that. I quietly smiled back at her. I then looked at Aishwarya and said with a grin, "Yeah, it's a spiritual thing."

An hour later, we stood at the gate, bidding goodbye and whatnot to the family. I leaned against my dad, resting my head against his shoulder. I yawned sleepily, my eyes almost closing. Voices were faint. I couldn't really figure out what anyone was saying. Last thing I remember, I was waving at them, and the next thing I knew, I opened my eyes and looked at the clock which showed 4 in the night.

I opened my eyes and sat up. I looked around, I was in my bed. Covers on, lights turned off. I rubbed my eyes and thought to myself, "Magic." I smiled a little and fell back, my head on my comfy pillow.

I dozed off, as Dhruv would put it, quoting John Green once again, "I fell in love with the way you fall asleep – slowly and then all at once."

five.

I walked downstairs, wearing my Beatles T-shirt, Superman pyjamas and my hair were all messed up. I reached the ground floor and mum was making some tea. I smiled and said, "Good morning, mother!" She turned around and replied, "Good morning, Nikita." I picked up an apple that was placed in a bowl on the counter table. I took a bite, a little of the juice sliding down the left corner of my mouth. I saw mum pouring the tea into two cups. She said, "My, my, look at you. Up so early today." I chewed a little, crossing my eyebrows lightly and replied, "Yeah, I have some errands to run." She nodded her head and asked, "Can I ask what those errands are?" I was about to say something, then my iPhone, which rested in my pyjamas' pocket, ringed. I put the apple down on the counter table and pulled out my iPhone. I picked it up immediately and spoke into the phone, "Yeah, Ashwini?"

I turned my back towards mum and spoke to Ashwini for a while before ending the conversation with, "Yeah, okay. I'll see you in, say… three hours. I have to make a run to Mini ma'am's place. Uh-huh. 'Kay." I hung up and slipped the phone back into my pocket. I turned around and saw mum looking at me with folded arms. She asked in an obvious tone, "Errands?" I gulped and replied, "Yeah, yeah. People got me running around and stuff. You know, the usual." She nodded once and said in her of-course-that-is-bloody-obvious tone, "Yeah, the usual." I smirked, picked up my apple and ran upstairs to my room.

I got ready for the day and it was 11 am. As I wore my Nike dunks, my iPhone ringed. I took it out of my pocket and Ashwini was calling. I picked it up and spoke into the phone while pressing it against my right shoulder, "Now what? I said three hours." She spoke back, "I know, I know. Make that four, please." I tied my shoelaces and asked, "Four? But why?"

"Just do that for me. I have some…err… work to take care of."

"You're not ditching on me with a boy, right?"

She shouted into the phone, "What? NO! Shut up, Nikita!"

"I'm kidding. Four hours, then. Good. I get some more time."

"More time for what?"

"Oh, I have some work to take care of."

She asked in a tone similar to mine, "You're not ditching on me with a boy, are you? Dhruv, maybe?" I put my feet down on the ground and replied, holding the phone to my ear, "No, I'm not. Shut your trap." She laughed into the phone and said, "I'll see you then. Ciao." She hung up and I shoved my phone into my jeans' pocket as I stood up. I walked towards the room's door and picked up my motor-gloves from the top of my books cabinet. I picked up my shoulder-sling bag and put it over my right shoulder. I walked out of the room and shut the door behind me. I walked down the stairs.

"Mum?" I shouted, looking around the lobby. I walked into the kitchen to get a bottle of water. I opened the fridge and shut it immediately, seeing a sticky note put on it. I pulled it off. It read, "Nikita, I'm going for my dental appointment. I'll call you once I'm done. Take care." I nodded once and tore the paper, tossing it into the dustbin. I took out a bottle of cool water from the fridge, uncapped it and took a quick drink, gulping down half of the bottle. I put it back in and shut the fridge. I scratched my cheek and walked out of the kitchen, then walked out of the house, shutting the main door behind me. I walked over to the garage and removed my Firefox from its stand. I pulled on both my gloves and walked my bike out of the main gate. I shut the main gate as I exited and I climbed my bike, riding out of our huge property.

I rode down a few blocks, riding through the marketplace. I increased the speed a little as I reached the main road. I pedalled down the road, crossing a cinema and a three-star hotel on the way. I slowed down as I took a turn around the corner into a broad street. I pedalled down and then took the third right. I slowed down as I reached Mini ma'am's place. I stopped in front of her house's gate. I got off my bike and rang the doorbell. I stretched my feet a little as I removed my gloves. I looked around as the sun shone brightly. My eyebrows lightly crossed as the sun fell directly on my face and the trees around failed to protect me from the sunlight.

I heard the gate open and I turned my eyes towards as I saw Sarah standing there, holding the gate's handle.

"Nikita," she said, through the little gap in the gate, in a not so amused voice. "What is, someone as incompetent as you, doing here?" I smirked unpleasantly and replied, "As much as disrespectful as that sounds, I would very much like to punch you in the face, but I won't." She raised her eyebrows, a little surprised on hearing the last three words. She asked, "You won't? You hate me, don't you?" I chuckled and replied, "I never lied to you, Sarah, because it doesn't serve me. And no, I don't hate you. Can't." She smiled a little, opening the gate, "Come on in." I smiled and walked my bike into the yard. I put it on the stand and walked after Sarah as she led me into her house. She stopped as I entered the lobby.

"Mum's not home, you know that, right?" Sarah said. I raised one of my eyebrows and asked, "Why didn't you tell me that before? Where is she, anyway?" Sarah ran a hand through her long brown hair and answered, "School work. I don't even know what. She didn't tell me." I nodded my head once and said in a cold voice, "Alright. Just give her this." I brought my bag to the front. Unzipping the main pocket, I took out a thick book and gave it to Sarah. She took it, looking at the book's cover, and asked, "Jeffery Archer?" I nodded once. She smiled and continued, "Mum loves Jeffery Archer. She thinks he's brilliant." I returned the smile as she looked up at me.

"Your mother and I share very similar opinions," I said. "I should get going now." Sarah nodded her head but offered to stay awhile. I shook my head slowly in denial and walked out of the house. "And yeah," I turned towards Sarah as I took my bike off its stand, "Ask her to call me once?" She held the book close and replied, "I will do that." I smiled and thanked her. She waved at me and I waved back as I walked my bike out the gate, shutting the gate behind me. The bike leaned against me as I put my gloves on, strapping them to their Velcro.

"Short trip?" asked a voice. I looked to my left and saw Mini ma'am standing there, locking her car's door. I smiled and said, "Hey." She walked up to me, circling the car key around her left index finger. She asked again, "What are you doing here?" I turned towards her, minding my bike from falling, and answered, "Just came to give you the Jeffery Archer book." She smiled happily, keeping her hand on her chest and said, "Aw, you came all the way for that? So sweet." I chuckled and said, jokingly, "Don't be too dramatic."

My iPhone vibrated. I took it out from my pocket and said to Mini ma'am, still looking at the phone's screen, "Ah, I'll have to catch you later now." I shoved the phone back into my pocket and continued, shrugging my shoulders, "Errands." She nodded and replied, "Of course. Ciao, Nikita." I smiled and mounted my bike. As I was about to leave, I stopped. I turned towards Mini ma'am, who was standing at the gate.

"Remember how you once said," I said, "when I stood 2nd in that Inter School English Debate, and the next day, I screwed up big time for something I cannot recall right now, and you were mad at me – remember how you said you wished we could start from page one?" She looked at me with seriousness in her eyes. I continued, gripping my bike's handle, "We could try if you still want to." She folded her arms and leaned against the black metallic gate. She asked, lightly crossing her eyebrows, "You think we could?" I looked away for a moment, then looked back at her and said with coolness in my voice, "There's always room for trial." She pressed her tongue against her left inner-cheek, then sighed and said, "I don't want to start from page one. Page one thousand-something is fine for me."

I smiled a little as she leaned forward to gently pat my cheek, and said, "You're a catastrophe, you know that?" I looked at her, gripped both the bike's handles, and replied, "I know that, yes." I sighed as she chuckled. I continued, "Well, too bad, so sad, hope I didn't make you mad."

Our gaze met and the two of us laughed. I waved and said, "See you later." She waved back as I turned my bike around.

I pedalled away.

six.

"I am telling you," I said to Ashwini as the two of us rode down the street, she on her scooty and I on my bike, alongside each other. "There is no way in hell you can win a video-game playoff against me." She rolled her eyes and replied as I pedalled, "I never said I could." I nodded my head and said, "Because you can't." She made a little frustrated noise and then said, "Forget about that. Let's play the classic Koffee with Karan Rapid Fire game." I nodded my head in approval. Ashwini smiled and said, "Potato."

"Ashwini Kamboj."

She gasped as I said that. I looked at her and chuckled. She said again, "Hot."

"Johnny Depp."

"Beautiful."

"Alan Shore in the courtroom."

"Legendary."

"Cillian Murphy."

"Chocolate."

"Lindt."

"Lips."

"Cillian Murphy."

She shook her head lightly and said in a low voice, "Pervert." I hit her leg with mine, since the distance between us was almost nothing, and said in an opposite tone to hers, "Next."

"Marriage."

"Not my cup of tea."

"Facebook."

"Admin."

"Twitter."

"That blue bird."

"The Beatles."

"Amazing."

"Poets of the Fall."

"Love of my life."

She sighed and said, "Okay, I'm done. I got nothing else on me." We turned right into another street, and she continued, "I seriously thought you'd be mad at me since I cancelled our plans for last night." I scratched the back of my head with one hand, the other hand gripping the handle of the bike, and replied, "Oh, I'm mad. I'm very mad at you." She looked at me as she drove and before she could say anything, I sang in Drake Bell's tune, "Well, too bad, so sad, hope I didn't make you mad!" Ashwini smiled and sang the next line, "I can't make you stop and listen, that won't save you."

"I can't believe!"

"Everybody wants to party all night long, till the birds are singing."

Then the two of us sang in one voice, in a high pitch, "So do what you wanna do! Be what you wanna be! Live like you wanna live, if you wanna be free, then you're gonna be free!"

I lost myself to the sound of those lines. I shut my eyes and sang, only the sound of Ashwini and my voice in my ears, "So say what you wanna say! Hear what you wanna hear! Live like you wanna live..." Ashwini then sang, her voice almost cracking, "...if you wanna be free, then you're gonna be free!" I looked at Ashwini and we laughed together. We set our eyes on the road.

I heard her scooty's engine rev up, and Ashwini drove a little ahead of me. She looked back and yelled, "Race you to your place!" I yelled back, a little on disadvantage, "This isn't even fair!" She looked back again and said, "Aw, is our little Nixter giving up?" I inflated my nostrils and said in an angry tone, "You're on!" She smiled at me and then set her eyes on the road. She raced in front of me. I pedalled very fast and tried to control the bike which wasn't that hard to handle. I pedalled a little more and gained speed and momentum. I caught up with Ashwini and now both of us were making our way up the down the narrow street, but Ashwini accelerated and took the lead. I grinned and said to myself, "Oh, screw this." I pedalled even faster and overtook her. I saluted Ashwini as I passed. Ashwini's mouth was open and she looked a little scared but I knew she wasn't. That girl drove her scooty at a speed of 100 km/h on the National Highway once! She wouldn't do it in the narrow lane, though. I created quite a gap between the two of us. I looked back at Ashwini, and smiled cockily, and yelled, "Who's awesome? I'm awesome!" I could see Ashwini's eyes widen. She yelled back, "Nikita! Look ahead!" I turned my head towards the front and saw a huge boulder in front of me. I braked as hard as I could, sliding both my feet on the ground, trying to stop the bike, but it was too late. I managed to lose speed but I hit the boulder. I fell over along with my bike, hitting my head against the bar-handle. I let out a groan as I landed there, my bike on top of me. My eyes were shut, the world around me drowned into utter silence. I opened my eyes as I heard Ashwini's voice in my ears.

I heard her say, "Nikita! Get up, for heaven's sake!" I looked up at her as she kneeled near me. I smiled a little, narrowing my eyes to focus, and said, almost whispered, "Hey, there." She put my bike away and helped me sit up. I sat up on the ground, folding one of my knees and the other to my face. I lifted my right arm with my left hand, holding it still. "Ouch," I said. Ashwini shook her head and said angrily, "Such an idiot. How are you feeling?" She ran her fingers around my right cheek. She continued, "You're bleeding." I sighed and replied cockily, "These wounds will heal, but the marks humans leave are too often scars." She slapped me lightly on my other cheek and said, "Such an idiot, still quoting John Green." I looked at my right elbow, which was bleeding, dirt around it, and then I said, "Speaking of scars..." Ashwini looked at me and I sang in my cold voice, "I tear my heart open, to sew myself shut. My weakness is that I care too much. And my scars remind me that the past is real..." I looked at Ashwini, who didn't look amused. I stopped singing and I looked down to the ground. She chuckled and continued the song, "I tear my heart open, just to feel." I looked at her, a sparkle in my eyes, and I laughed. She stood up and reached her hand out.

"Come on," she said. "Let's get your dad to see how much the damage really is."

I looked at her, my eyes full of contentment. I took her hand and stood up, dusting the dirt off my right elbow carefully.

seven.

Dad examined my wound and applied some ointment on it. I rebounded a little as the ointment burned the wound. Dad looked at me and asked, "Burns?" I nodded once. He continued, "Well, take care not to fall down next time." I looked at him and nodded again, without saying a word. I looked at Ashwini, who sat on the chair kept next to mine. Ashwini smiled. My dad looked at Ashwini as he capped the ointment, and said, "Thank you, Ashwini." She stood up as soon as he completed his sentence, and she said, "Oh, it's nothing, uncle. Nikita's my best friend. It's the least I could do for her." I smiled as she said that. I slowly ran my hand over the wounds on my face which had stopped bleeding now. Ashwini then continued, "I should get going now. I have work to get done." She looked at me and leaned forward, whispering in my ear, "Take care of yourself." I nodded my head. She pulled back and said in her normal pitch, "And your bike's in the garage. See you later, uncle." My father smiled at her as she walked out of his cabin.

I pushed back into the chair, putting my head back, staring at the ceiling, I sighed. Dad sat into his revolving chair and asked, "Feel alright?" I looked at him and nodded once. He chuckled and said, "You can speak, you know. I won't kill you." I opened my mouth and said in a low pitch, "I thought you would." He played with the paperweight on his table and said, a quiet smile on his face, "I wouldn't, no, no. We all get hurt." I looked at him, looking forward to what he'd say next. He continued, "I used to fall off my bike all the time when I was your age."

"Seriously?" I asked.

"Seriously. This one time... I actually crashed my bike into a haystack. I ended up in the haystack. And I was so scared. No one came to help because no one was around. I walked home all by myself, a limp in my walk."

I don't know why, but I burst out laughing as he completed the sentence. He laughed along and continued, "And my parents were very strict. I wasn't allowed to go out all by myself after that, for about a month or something." I chuckled and asked, a slight husk in my voice, "And you still remember all this?" He nodded his head, quivering his lips, and said, "You'll remember this..." He pointed towards my elbow and cheek. "...as well." I smiled a little and stood up.

"I should get home now," I said.

"Of course. Tell your mother not to worry too much."

"I'll tell her that."

I was about to walk out of his cabin, but stopped as he said, "Nikita." I turned around and looked at him. He continued, "You're very lucky to have a friend like Ashwini." I flicked my hair back and replied cockily, "She should be the lucky one." My dad smiled as I said that. I smiled back and said, bowing my head a little, "Thanks, dad."

He gave me thumbs up and gestured his assistant to bring in the next patient. I walked out of his cabin.

eight.

I walked back home, which was connected to the hospital. I knocked on the door and mum opened it after a moment. I dropped my head slightly and looked at her with my puppy eyes. She rolled her eyes and said, opening the door, "Get in." I walked in, a slight limp in my walk. She shut the door behind me and just as I was about to sneak back up to my room, she stopped me, "Hold it." I sighed deeply and turned around to face her. Before she could say anything, I said, trying to grasp sympathy, speedily, "I'm sorry, mum, I will ne'er ever race Ashwini again. Heck, I won't race anyone ever again. That's a promise! I'll sign a contract if you want, just please don't ground me! Please, mum, please!" I joined my hands together. She replied, eyes wide open, "Okay, okay, calm it, Nikita. You're not grounded." I sighed satisfactorily and dropped my shoulders and said with a smile, "Thanks, mum, you won't regret it." She smirked and replied, "I'd better not." I looked at her, a little scared, then nodded and walked back up to my room.

Just as I got to my room, my iPhone rang. I swanked it out of my pocket and without even seeing who was calling, I answered and spoke into the phone, not too charmingly, "Whoever this is, I am not in the mood to talk, okay?" As I was about to hang up, I heard Dhruv yell into his phone, "Nikita Achanta! How dare you crash your bike? Are you alright? You're not hurt, are you?" I sighed deeply and spoke back, "News travels fast, yes?" He got back to his normal pitch and said, "Yeah, I was just passing by Ashwini's house and she told me."

"That jackass."

"And, err..."

"What?"

"I kind of told... Lakshita..."

I completed his sentence, "And now that she knows, everyone knows. Good. Charming." Dhruv sighed and replied, "I'm sorry."

"Don't sweat it. It's fine, really. What else do I have to do today?"

"What are you planning to do?"

"Sit in bed, order some pizza, listen to some music, and watch Red Eye or Red Lights or any other Murphy movie.... And maybe breathe."

He stifled a laugh and replied, "Breathe. Breathing is good. I'll come by later, maybe, okay?" I nodded my head once and said, "Works for me."

"Take care now, okay?"

"Okay."

"And don't walk or exert yourself too much."

"Done."

"And remember to take your medicine on time."

"Will do."

"And don't forget to catch up on lost sleep. You need sleep."

"Mm-hmm."

"And make sure not to—"

"Alright, fine, I get it! God, you sound so much like my mother."

"I'm not even sure if that's a compliment."

"My mum is the best mum in the world, that's a huge compliment."

"Aw, Nikita, I—"

"Oh, just suck it up and hang up already."

"Take care, okay?"

"Okay."

"Hey," he said into the phone. "Maybe 'okay' could be our 'always'."

That made me laugh. I chuckled and said, "The Augustus Waters to my Hazel Grace? Some other day, maybe."

He laughed a little as I hung up and chucked the phone on my bed.

It was 2 in the night. I lay in my bed, covers on, lights all off, my Bose headphones over my ears and my iPod's screen in front of my face, the light shining over me. I played Temple Run 2, making a score of about 17 million in one run. I yawned as I put my iPod next to my pillow and listened to Linkin Park. I shut my eyes and listened to "Breaking The Habit" as I dozed off.

A few moments later, I found myself tumbling through nothingness. Then, all of a sudden, out of nowhere, BAM! I held an M25 sniper in my hands. I wore a black overcoat and a pair of black jeans, gloves covering both my hands and shades over my eyes. I stood on a rooftop. It seemed like it was some time in the evening. I leaned down and saw a lady with long dark brown hair, wearing an overcoat and a muffler around her neck, holding a cup of coffee in her hand. I cocked the M25, setting it very carefully and precisely. I aimed for her head. I shut my left eye as I looked through the marker for precision. I held the gun firmly, my right hand's finger on the trigger. I sighed once and held my breath for a moment as I pressed the trigger. The bullet went rushing through the air, only to enter the lady's skull. I sighed as she fell to the ground. I looked down and had a tear escape my right eye. I was about to turn around but I felt a sudden entrance into my back. I looked to my chest and it was covered with blood. I fell to my knees, putting my hand to the wound, and I dropped dead.

And that was all I remembered the next day.

nine.

The next day, I woke up a little early because of the freakish nightmare the night before. I sat in my bed and looked around as I tried to find myself again. I hugged myself as I felt a sudden chill down my back. I breathed heavily, a little scared. I felt a little pain in my chest. I buried my face in my hands, shutting my eyes tight, and then ran both my hands through my hair. I looked to my bedside table and the clock showed 7 in the morning.

"Too early," I said to myself. I sighed, looked at the ceiling once, and then crashed back on the bed. I rolled over to the other side, trying to keep my hurt elbow safe, and closed my eyes, trying to get back on lost sleep.

four hours later...

I sat on my chair, flipping my pen, trying to write a poem. I yawned as my train of thought carried me away. I leaned back into the chair because I could not think of how to sum up that nightmare into a poem. I stretched my body, sending chills down my spine and almost a little cramp.

71

"Ouch," I said to myself. I rested my right elbow on the chair's arm and flipped my pen between my fingers. I then rested my head against my fist and shut my eyes and let out a long sigh.

"Big sigh," said a familiar voice from behind. I turned around in my revolving chair and Ashwini was standing there, leaning against the door. I asked out of surprise, "What are you doing here?" She walked a little forward and shoved her hands into her jeans' pockets, and said, "Was bored, thought you'd be doing something interesting." I shook my head and sighed again. She chuckled and repeated her sentence, "Big sigh." I nodded once and replied, "Yeah, I've sighed bigger." I got up from my chair and sighed again. Ashwini raised an eyebrow and asked, "Why are you sighing so much?" I looked at her and replied, my vocalization irritated, "I do what I want!" I ran my hands through my hair and walked out to the balcony. Ashwini followed and asked as I leaned against the railing, "What happened?" I looked at the open and clear sky and replied, "Terrible nightmare. I'll be fine." She leaned next to me and licked her lips and said, "Alright. I believe you." I looked at her and smirked, then looked away and sang, "I don't wanna be another wave in the ocean..." Ashwini chuckled and continued, "I am a rock, not just another grain of sand!" I looked at her and sang in the song's tune, "Wanna be the one you run to when you need a shoulder...." Our gaze met and she sang, "I ain't a soldier but I'm here to take a stand..." The two of us smiled widely and sang together, "Because we can!" The two of us laughed lightly and then looked to the trees at a distance. Ashwini sighed happily and said, "You can sing that song at the farewell." I crossed my eyebrows and looked at her, "Farewell? 10th grade never has a farewell."

"Well, they are this year. Next week. I was at school an hour back. I'm hosting."

"Wow. That's...that's great."

I looked away, my look turned serious. Ashwini looked at me and bit her lip, then said, "Someone's jealous." I looked at her and replied in my cold voice, "I am not jealous. Why would I be jealous? Of you, of all people?"

"Because they didn't ask you to host."

"I don't even care. I'm done with that school forever. So it doesn't really matter."

"Or maybe it does. Because you're attached to the school."

I averted my gaze and spoke, "I am not attached. Not to the school, not to anyone." Ashwini folded her arms against the railing and said, her tone a little suppressed, "Really, now. Whom are you trying to fool? Your best friend? You're failing, then." I stifled a laugh and replied, "Who fools a fool anyway?" I grinned and Ashwini's jaw dropped. She sighed and said, "Yeah, okay, whatever." I tapped my fingers gently on the railing. I brushed my hair away from my forehead and then asked, trying not to sound too desperate, "So... there are going to be performances at this farewell?" Ashwini nodded once, "Yep. Tons of them. Your performance is the last one." I looked at her and shook my head as I spoke, "I'm not going to perform. Not in front of the entire batch of 10th and teachers who don't appreciate English music. I'm not going to, Ash." I looked away.

"Come on, Nikita. You're going away. The last thing you can do is blow everyone off their feet."

"Well, I'm not going to sing for any of them. Know why?"

"Why?"

"Because I hate everyone. Who knows that better than you?"

"You don't hate everyone. Now, don't lie."

"Ashwini..."

She stopped me before I could say anything further. She stood straight and spoke as I folded my arms and leaned against the railing, "Look. You don't hate all of them. I know that. And even if you do, some of them care about you. You know, I'm one of them. And I care about you. So much. And there are other people too. Dhruv. Lakshita. So, if not for yourself..." I looked at her and she continued, "...do it for the people who care about you. Because I know, that in the end, they're going to miss you. Much more than you think they will. I just... And you're attached to them too, even if you wish to deny that." I sighed and buried my face in the groove created by my folded arms. I then looked at her and said in a low voice, "I'm still going to stick to my opinion, Ash," I shook my head and corrected myself, "I don't do 'feelings'. So unlike me." Ashwini folded her arms and laughed lightly, "Right. Of course. Why not." I looked at her as she continued, her voice all serious, the happiness gone from her face, "Our ability to feel pain, anger, sorrow, anxiety, happiness, is what makes us all human. You might act like that one person who is cold on the inside and the outside, but you're not. Who knows it better than me?" I looked away and nipped at my upper lip. Ashwini sighed and I said, "I'm going to go do some of mum's work. Do you mind?" I shook my head but said nothing. Ashwini whispered, "I'll leave you to your thoughts, then." She turned around as I looked at her. She nodded her head and turned around, waving, and said, "I'll see you later, Nikita." I watched her walk away. I sighed deeply and looked up at the sky again and saw an eagle fly by.

"I want to break free," I sighed, shutting my eyes tightly. "Please."

ten.

"Mum, mum, mum," I shouted across the lobby as I rushed down the stairs. "Mum?" I jumped to the ground from the last few stairs.

"Yes, Nikita?" My mum spoke from the kitchen.

I leaned against the countertop and said, "Our school's having a farewell for class tenth. Next week—" Before I could continue, mum handed me a letter, it's envelope bearing the seal of our school. "Here," she said as I took it from her. I tore open the envelope and read it out to her.

Dear Miss Nikita Achanta,

Your school, Sant Nischal Singh Public School, would happily like to invite you to the class tenth farewell next week. The whole batch is requested to be present for one last gathering. All teachers and the batch of 9th grade will also be present. There will be several performances and phones and cameras are allowed. No specific dress-code. We hope to see you there. In fact, we'd love to see you there.

The principal on behalf of the staff and trust.

"Wow!" my mum exclaimed with a smile on her face. I put the letter back on the countertop and said, "Not as grand as you think it's going to be." As I looked down at the letter placed on the countertop, she sighed and said, "Nikita, this is the last time you get to see all your friends and teachers. You'll have fun, I can guarantee that." I scratched my cheek and replied, "I hope."

I turned around and sat on the marble stairs. I sighed under my breath and pulled my iPhone out of my pocket. I unlocked it by entering a complex password and then texted Ashwini.

> I'll do it. That closing performance. I'm up for it. – NA.

I waited for her to reply. After a minute, my iPhone played an Assassin's Creed ringtone and I received a text.

> I knew you'd accept it. It's why you're awesome and why I have high hopes and expectations of you. Always do. Show up for rehearsal tomorrow at school, around 10 am. See ya, buddy. - AK.

I smiled and looked up at mum. She had her glasses on and was doing something on her BlackBerry.

"Mum?" I said.

She had her eyes fixed on her phone's screen and asked, "Hmm?"

I tapped my fingers on my knees and replied, "I'm performing at the farewell." She looked at me through her glasses and said with a smile, "Wonderful! What are you doing?" I folded my legs and replied, pouting my lips slightly, "A set of songs, I don't know which ones yet, though." I stood up and continued, "I'll get

back to you on that one, after tomorrow's rehearsal."
She smiled sweetly and said, "Lovely." I smiled back
and walked up to the couch, jumping on to it from the
back. I got up and then walked up to the TV, turning
on the system and then turned on the Xbox. I put in the
CD of FIFA 13 and picked up the controller and jumped
back on to the black couch. I selected FC Barcelona as
my team and set up a match against Real Madrid, one
team that I hated quite a lot. I clicked 'Play Match' and
the match started.

"Dribble."

"Sprint."

"Tackle. Not too hard."

"Sliding tackle, now."

"That wasn't even offside! What even—?"

"Pass left to Fabregas."

"Dribble, Messi, dribble."

"Pass to Villa."

"Now, pass back to Messi."

"Aaaaaaand…"

"Shoot!"

I shook my fist as a sign of victory as I scored the
first goal, difficulty level set at Professional. At the
end of the 90th minute, I won the game, the score 4-3.
I sighed happily and after a second, my phone rang,
playing 'Demons' by Imagine Dragons. I took it out of
my pocket and without looking at the caller ID, picked it
up and spoke into the phone, "Achanta here." A friendly
and extrovert voice spoke back, "Been a while, Nikita."
I put the controller to the side and gripped the phone to

my ear. I crossed my eyebrows lightly and asked, "May I know who this is?"

"Funny you forget your cousins so fast."

"Uh..."

"It's Samira, you idiot."

"Ah, hey, Samira. Sorry, my brain's a little clogged these days. Anyway, it's been too long, huh?"

"It sure has been! But I'll be seeing you soon."

"I'm sorry, but I'm not coming to Bangalore any time soon."

"Not you, silly. I'm coming to your place!"

"You are?"

"Yeah, I have a flight tomorrow morning. Then I have some work in Delhi, so I'll probably reach your place by... say... 9 in the night."

"That's... uh... that's great!"

"I can't wait to see you and uncle and aunty. It's going to be wonderful!"

"Sure will be. I'll see you then? I'm a little busy right now."

"Oh, of course. Take care, kiddo. I'll see you tomorrow."

I nodded my head slightly and forced a smile. I then hung up and held my phone in my hand. I sighed deeply and buried my face in my hands. Samira was one cousin of mine whom I wasn't too friendly with, neither did we speak much. She and I had nothing in common and I hadn't seen her in three years. There was bound to be some sort of awkward conversation between the two of us, I was sure about it. I called out; my face still buried in my hands, "Mum?" She spoke from the kitchen, "Yes?" I looked up at the TV screen and said, "Samira's coming tomorrow." I stood up and faced the kitchen as she spoke, "Really? Lovely!" I shoved my hands into my jeans' pockets and replied, "For you. You know I don't like her, neither do I appreciate her and I sharing the same room." I saw my mum pour some milk into a glass, and she said, "Oh, balderdash and piffle, Nikita. I'm sure you'll have a lot to talk about. It's been three years since you last met." I chuckled and replied, "My life's been peaceful. Till now." Mum turned towards me and said, "Oh, Nikita. Anyway, you're going to take her out for some coffee day after, okay?" My jaw dropped slightly and I asked, "But why?! Why me?" She walked up to me and said a little seriously, "You two need to bond. Besides, you're going to lie in bed all day, anyway. Do something productive, yes?" I shook my head lightly and replied, giving up to her, "Alright, fine. I'll try not to hurt myself." My mum laughed lightly and nodded once. I picked up the remote from the centre table and turned the TV off. I walked past her and said, "I'm going to be in my room. Call me if you need me." I was about to walk off, but then I turned around and continued, "Don't need me." I walked up to my room and shut the door behind me. I sighed again and ran my hands through my hair, thinking off what I'd talk to Samira about. The two of us had absolutely nothing in common.

I hated socialising with almost everyone, may it be some complete stranger or someone I passed by every day. I just hated everyone so much, even if Ashwini tried to change my mind, trying to convince me that I didn't hate everyone. I often denied myself to the fact that there was actually hope for humanity and mankind. But seeing people every day, the evil that men do and how screwed up society actually is, made me deny the fact and I knew that there'd never be any hope for society, unless and until someone like Mahatma Gandhi stepped on this godforsaken earth. Then again, that wasn't going to happen because no one had the ability, or the capacity, to see the good. No one, including me, wanted to search for the truth, or promote the power of truth. Society's made up of lies, greed, anger and hatred. Nothing more. It's what I've always believed in.

As Dhruv would say, quoting John Green, "If people were rain, I was drizzle and she was a hurricane."

eleven.

"She's not all that bad, you know," said Ashwini, as the two of us walked around the school building with two cups of coffee in each of our hands.

"Oh, please," I said. "You only say that because you haven't met her in, like, forever." Ashwini took a sip of her coffee. She held some files in her other hand, because she was the host. She replied, "There's good in everyone, Nikita. I still don't get it as to why you choose to overlook the goodness in people." I said a little sarcastically, "Uh, maybe because everyone's so screwed over that they actually hide the goodness in them somewhere so deep, where even their gurus can't find it. Everyone lies every day. And since I'm such a pessimist, maybe I can't look at the 'good' they hide within themselves." I stopped walking and looked at Ashwini as she pressed the coffee cup with 'I love coffee' written over it, against her lips, and I asked, "Can you look at the good they hide within?" She looked at me and coughed slightly, bringing the cup away from her lips, she said, "Maybe I can. Maybe I can't. But I can certainly see the good in you; no matter how much of a pessimist you are or how much you hate everyone, even if you're an atheist, I know there's good to you." I laughed lightly and replied,

"You talk like you're Sherlock who's trying to talk Moriarty out of a bank robbery or something. Well, you know what?" She pressed her lips together and then asked, "What?" I leaned in close and spoke close to her face, my voice almost a whisper, "Before Sherlock can even try to talk Moriarty out of it, Moriarty's already done it. So what I'm saying is..." I pulled back and continued, "...don't try to find the good in me. You'll get lost." I smirked and walked to the school's main ground. Ashwini followed but said nothing.

We reached the school's ground and all of the performers for the farewell had gathered there. Being the host that she was, Ashwini climbed on to the stage by the stairs and spoke into the mike, "Can everyone hear me?" The whole of the crowd nodded and Ashwini continued, "Brilliant. Okay, guys, so we're going to begin with the rehearsals now." She flipped open one of the files and took continued to speak into the mike as she read from the piece of paper, "Okay, first act we have is Zenia and Zeeshan, performing Michael Jackson's 'Smooth Criminal'. You two, up on the stage, now." Ashwini turned off the mike and got off the stage as the Zs climbed on.

Ashwini came and stood next to me, her coffee cup still in her hand. I took a sip of my coffee and sang, "You've been hit by, you've been struck by a smooooooth criminal!" She chuckled and whispered, "I don't know the lyrics to that song, Nikita." I looked at her and whispered back, "I was actually singing in context to Jim Moriarty." She shook her head lightly, her eyes fixed on the two performers, "You and your obsessions."

I laughed lightly and wrapped an arm around her shoulder. I then said, "Can't say you won't miss them." I looked to the stage as the rehearsals began. Ashwini looked at me as I completed the sentence. Her expressions gone blank. She gulped slightly and then looked to the stage, she said nothing.

twelve.

an hour later...

I sat on one of the chairs at the back, flicking through photos of Ben Whishaw on my iPhone. I had my feet resting on the back of a chair in front of me. I sat with a toothpick placed in between my lips and I was gently playing with the ring on my left index finger as I silently fangirled over Ben's perfection. I sighed dreamily, but was interrupted when I felt a tap on my shoulder. I turned my neck and Mini ma'am was standing there. She smiled and said, "Hey." I smiled back and replied, "Hey to you too." She pulled a chair and sat next to me, folding her legs. I scratched my nose and put my iPhone on standby and shoved it into my jeans' pocket. I sighed as I looked towards the stage. Mini ma'am asked, her voice a whisper, "Liking the performances?" I looked at her and chuckled, then replied sarcastically, "Loving them." She bit her lower lip and said, "You really do hate everything, huh?" I nodded my head quickly, then shook my fist and replied, "Pessimist for life, lady."

"So I heard your performance is the last of the evening."

"Yes, it is."

"Why? You're usually the opening performer. It's just weird. Slightly different."

I looked at her and then narrowed my eyes, starting to make sense of the words that escaped her lips.

"You're right," I said. "I'm the one who blows away the night. Why is it different this time?" I looked around and saw Ashwini standing near the stage and talking to one of her friends. I shouted out, "Hey, Ashwini!" She looked around and then looked at me. I gestured her to come meet me. She carefully and gently made her way through the crowd. She nodded once and said with a smile, "Good to see you, Mini ma'am." She sat on a seat next to me. I looked at her and asked in a low voice, "Why's my performance last? Nixter never performs last. You know that well." She nodded her head once and replied in the same pitch, "Yeah, I know, that's why I want you to perform a song you truly love. Something you hold close to your heart." I still had the toothpick in my mouth. I silently chewed on its end and said to her seriously, "Really? And exactly which song do you want me to sing?"

"Some song you hold dear, dear."

"I hold tons of songs dear. You don't expect me to choose from all those, right?"

"Please, Nikita. For me. Do it for me, okay? Good girl."

I sighed as Ashwini stood up from her chair. She held the files close to her chest and then said, "Hey, Nikita?" I looked up at her and so did Mini ma'am. Ashwini smiled slightly and moved her hands in a dance step, and sang, "Ah, ah, ah, ah, stayin' alive!" She smiled and then walked away. I sighed happily and then said, as I looked at Mini ma'am, "Staying alive. It's just so boring, isn't it? It's just...staying." She nodded and gently patted my hand which rested on my knee, and replied, "Come on. You know how this life is." I nodded once and chewed on my lower lip, and said, "Suckish. It's a bittersweet symphony, this life. Trying to make ends meet, you're a slave to money, and then you die." She chuckled, "That's about it. So suck it up." I stretched my hands while sitting in my chair, and said, "Like I have another choice. Speaking of unfair things..." She looked at me and I continued, "...my cousin is coming to town tonight, and..." Before I could complete my sentence, Mini ma'am interrupted and asked, "Whoa, whoa, wait. You have tons of cousins. Which one is this?" I leaned both my arms and held my hands together on the left arm of the chair, got closer to her and whispered in my cold voice, "No, no, no. The other cousins, all the guys, I like all of them, because they're cool. Although this one..." I sighed deeply and Mini ma'am asked, yet again, "What about this one?"

"We don't get along well. And, well, she practically hates everything about me."

"Why would anyone hate you? You're totally awesome."

"Why, thank you," I said as a smile tugged my lips.

"Why does she hate you, anyway?"

"She doesn't hate me, more like she hates stuff about me. Like my tendency to fall in love with celebrities and fictional characters, or why I'm an atheist. She doesn't appreciate what I'm made of. Really."

"That's barbaric."

"I know. Crazy, too. And mum said that I have to take her for coffee tomorrow and 'socialise'."

"Now, now, we aren't very good at socialising, are we now?"

"No. I'm the worst. I just hate everyone and everything so much right now."

"Everything?" She looked into my eyes, nudging my arm lightly.

I looked back into her eyes and replied, "Muggles. I hate muggles. I don't hate you. No." I shook my head slightly. She chuckled and asked again, "Okay. So I'm a witch. Half-blood or...?"

"I'd say half-blood, because technically, I think your mum would have been muggle-born."

"Why?"

"Because... she... err... Okay, I just saw that in a dream, can we just leave it there?"

"Hah, alright then. So which house do I get sorted into, Miss Potterhead?"

"Hmm," I leaned back into my chair and looked up at the open sky. "Which house would you belong to? That's a tough one." I then looked at her and continued, speaking like a total Harry Potter wiz that I was, "I don't actually know because you fit into all. As fierce and brave as a Gryffindor. As cunning and ambitious and mysterious as a Slytherin. As loyal and totally adorable as a Hufflepuff. As smart, badass and intelligent as a Ravenclaw."

She tucked her hair behind her right ear and smiled up at me. I half-smiled and said, "You're multi-housed." She nodded her head and asked, "So I'm a Gryff..." I nodded quickly and completed the sentence, "You're a Gryff-Sly-Uffle-Claw, yeah." She giggled and said, "That's so cute, that sounds so cute." I replied cockily, "Only because I'm saying it. But I do wish you were a Slytherin." She stopped giggling and asked, again, "Because I'm as mysterious as the dark side of the moon?" I leaned forward and answered, "No, because I'm a Slytherin." I winked at her and then stood up from my chair. I stretched my body and asked, "Can I get you some coffee?" She looked up at me, her hand to her forehead; she twitched her eyes slightly due to the fierce sunlight, and asked, "Since when do we have coffee in school? We usually get by with tea." Running a hand through my hair and gently tugging at the ends, I replied, "Since these rehearsals started. I installed a coffeemaker in the staff room. You know I can't go even a day without caffeine intake." She laughed lightly and said, "And you got permission for that. Impressive." I shoved my hands into my pockets and replied modestly, "I didn't get permission. Ashwini did. That's what comes of being a teacher's pet." Mini ma'am nodded her head and said in a tone unlike hers, "You're a teacher's pet too. She is a principal's pet." I looked at her, raising my eyebrows slightly, I replied in the same tone, "You really should be in Slytherin." The two of us laughed together. I scratched my left cheek and said, "I'll catch you later." She smiled widely and replied, "You will."

I smiled and walked away.

thirteen.

It was 2 in the afternoon and the rehearsals were still going on. I stood next to the coffee machine in the staff room, waiting for my coffee to get ready. I yawned and then sighed. I was bored out of my mind. And then, behold, Ashwini walked in, like she had nothing better to do.

"Really now," she said in a what-is-wrong-with-you kind of tone. "What is that, your tenth cup of coffee this day?"

I looked at her and then at the coffee machine. I shook my head very fast and said, "No, no, no, ten is an exaggeration. That's my fifth cup."

"Oh, Nikita, can you not?"

"Dude, I can't help feeling unfitting around people I don't care about."

"So you don't feel fitting around anyone, huh?"

"That's one way to put it."

I took the coffee off the machine and poured into my cup with 'I need an extra doze on Mondays' engraved on it. I turned the machine off and took a sip of my coffee.

"Ah!" I exclaimed. "Just what I needed."

I was about to take another sip when Ashwini grabbed my sleeve and dragged me out of the staff room, "Jesus, come with me now." I felt a little jerk and the coffee almost fell over me. I almost yelled, "Hey, watch it, jerk." She rolled her eyes and walked to the ground, my shirt's sleeve still clutched. The rehearsals were still going on. She gently pushed me on to a chair and said angrily, "Will you please give me the list of songs you're going to perform at the farewell?" I pulled my shirt's sleeve down, wiping off the creases. I put my left leg over my right knee, cupping the cup in my hands, I replied with a smirk, "Let it be a surprise." I brought the cup up to my lips, but as I did, she took hold of my Barcelona jersey's collar, pushed my hand away lightly, and spoke close to my face, "If you do not give me the list ASAP, I'll have a surprise waiting for you. And it won't be nice." I looked at the hand that gripped my collar and then I looked into her eyes, and whispered, "Not the collar." She frowned and let go. I pulled my shirt down and set the collar right. She stood straight and looked away, folding her arms. I got up from the chair and took a sip of my coffee.

"Fine," I said blankly. "I'll text you the list." She looked at me, her eyes lit up, and replied, "I knew you'd come to." I narrowed my eyes slightly and moved a little forward and spoke close to her face, "The collar you held? You're going to pay for that." She backed off slightly and chuckled, a slight fright in her voice. I smirked and said, "I'm out of here." I was about to walk past her but she stood in front of me and said, almost pleading, "No, no, please stay. N-not for the rehearsals, but talk to me. I'm sick of this already." I looked at her and grinned unpleasantly, "The hosting job?" I patted her shoulder and continued, "Chill. I've seen bigger, and much worse. Ciao." I walked past her and she grabbed my arm and pulled me close, and whispered, "Okay, fine, not the rehearsal, just talk to me, about anything." I sighed and looked around and then looked at Ashwini as she flashed her puppy eyes and pouted slightly.

"Puppy eyes?" I asked, "Really, now?"

She nodded her head, still holding up the widened eyes and pout. I pulled up my sleeve and looked at my watch my friend got me from London. I pulled my sleeve down and said, "Ten minutes, then I'm out of here." She pulled back to her normal expressions and clapped happily. I chuckled and asked, "So what do you want to talk about?"

"What are your thoughts when you look at photos of Cillian Murphy?"

"That's just... just... no, you don't want to know that."

"I do, I do! Swear I won't judge you or anything."

"Dude, you can't judge a fangirl."

"Yeah, yeah. Please?"

"Swear you won't call me a pervert or something?"

"Cross my heart, and hope to die."

"Well..." I sighed. "Goddamn it, Cillian. Oh, dear God. Please. I love him and his Irishness and his eyes and his hair and his lips and his everything. Oh, shut up. That very awkward moment when I don't know what to do to myself because of how damn attractive he is. Welcome to my bed. Aw, shit. His jaw line, though. I want you so bad. Goddamn, you and your sweaters. This will always be so sexy. Oh, dear God, yes."

"Dude, really? Wow. Life of a fangirl sounds interesting." She stifled a laugh.

"I clearly have issues."

"I realised that when you said you wanted to drown yourself in a pool of coffee."

I looked at her all weird and said seriously, "I never said that, not to you at least." She averted her gaze and shifted her eyes from here to there and then replied, a little unsure, "Well…" I folded my arms and gave her a stern look, and asked, "You went through my conversations on my iPhone, didn't you? I sent that to Lakshita!" She answered a little nervously, "I just thought—" I interrupted her and said a little angrily, "I am never letting you lay hands on my iPhone ever again. I'm going to change the password as soon as I get home." She rolled her eyes and turned her back towards me, and said, "Are your ten minutes up?"

I bit into my cheek and said to myself, almost chuckling, "Unbelievable."

I shoved my hands into my pockets and walked off.

fourteen.

I put my bike on its stand in our garage and then walked into our house, shutting the door behind me. I saw my mum sitting on the lazy boy, her eyes glued to her Sony Vaio's screen.

"Hi, mum," I said.

She turned her head around slightly and said, "Hey. How was rehearsal?" I leaned against the couch next to the lazy boy and answered, letting out a sigh, "Boring. I did nothing." She nodded her head, not caring much, and got back to whatever she was doing on her laptop. "Oh, by the way," I said, leaning forward and flashing my coffee mug in front of her eyes, "Five cups of coffee. Apologies." She gave me a firm but gentle look, and asked, "Wait a minute. You actually installed the coffee machine at school?" I nodded my head, pulling the cup back, and answered, "I'm a girl of my words, mother." She chuckled and then looked at her laptop screen. I smiled a little and then was about to walk up to my room. I kept the coffee mug on the dining table and climbed two steps up the stairs, but then stopped. I looked at my mum as her back faced me, and I asked, "When's Samira coming again?"

"She'll reach here by, say, 9 or 10."

"Ah. Good, I'll be eating out tonight then."

"Out where?"

"Dominos', duh. I'll ask Ashwini to accompany me. Or Dhruv. Oh, I know! I'll just ask Ash, Lex, Dex, and Naaz to come have pizza with me at Dominos'. Perfect. Thanks, mum!"

"Uh... for what?"

"Oh, forget it."

I hurried up the stairs and up to my room. I shut the door behind me and pulled out my iPhone from my pocket. I opened the Whatsapp app and sent a group message to our group of five, 'Maybe best friends'. Don't ask about the group name. Dhruv came up with it. He sucks at naming. Anyway, I sent the following text:

Pizza at Dominos' tonight. My treat. –NA

After a few minutes, as I lay on my bed, my iPhone vibrated. I picked it up from the top of my stomach and unlocked it by entering a complex password. I scrolled through the Whatsapp conversations and opened the 'Maybe best friends' one.

Pizza sounds lovely! See you there. –DJ
Oh please, Dhruv, pizza sounds brilliant. We'll see you then. What time? –LJ
Yes, pizza! I don't have to put up with South Indian food tonight! Time? –NK
There has to be a catch behind this, Nixter. What's up? –AK

I groaned and shook my head at Ashwini's reply. I typed and sent:

95

Bloody brilliant. Naaz, Lex, Dex, I love you three. Ash?
I'm not so sure if I love you right now. And there's no
catch behind this, you jerk. By the way, 8's alright?
Or earlier? –NA

Since all four of them were online at the same time,
they replied.

8 it is! See you. I have work to do now. Bye! –NK
Whatever's good for you, Nikita. –DJ
Ashwini, stop being a meanie and suck it up. I'll see
you, Nixter. Bye. –LJ
God, you guys! Alright then. Seeeeeee ya. –AK

I chuckled slightly as I went through the
conversation again. I leaned back into my pillow and
sighed happily, thinking to myself, "Yes, so I'll avoid
a little of the unnecessary conversation with Samira
when she arrives. And Ashwini? You know me too well,
buddy. But I do want to spend time with you four. You
guys are my best friends. I wish you could read my
mind, though." I narrowed my eyes slightly and shook
my head, continuing thinking to myself, "No, scratch
that. Not my entire mind. The shallow thoughts, only.
Not the deeper ones. Those are… those are… hush, hush,
private." I chuckled and closed my eyes, sighing slowly
this time as my train of thought carried me away.

Vivid thoughts came to my mind.

"Cillian Murphy is wow."

"Dear Ben Whishaw, please stop with your
adorableness. You're killing me."

"Lovely smile, Tom Cruise!"

"Can we just skip to the part where I meet someone who's as much as a Potterhead as me?"

"Wait a minute..."

And then, my thoughts took a different turn and drifted away.

"Why on earth would Sarah invite me to her birthday party?"

"There's a catch behind this, isn't there?"

"Shut up, Nikita, stop thinking like Ashwini!"

"But what if there is? What if she wants to poison me and kill me and then steal all of my writing work and claim it all for herself?"

"Nikita. Shut. Up. As long as her mother cares about you, Sarah would never do that. And Sarah is a big fan of yours, she just doesn't admit it."

"Yeah, I guess I'm just a pessimist."

"That you are."

"So... I'm talking to myself again?"

"You're talking to Nixter, not yourself."

"You talk like I'm Jonathan Crane and you're Scarecrow, my alter-ego."

"You never know."

"Dude, you and I are one person, and what am I even saying? Snap out, snap out, snap out...now!"

I opened my eyes all of a sudden and sat up on my bed.

Whoa," I said to myself. "My head really is messed up. I really am a mess." I smiled slowly and continued, "I'm so proud. This messiness is my organisation."

fifteen.

I walked happily down the stairs, wearing my Levi's jeans, a shirt with the Batman symbol on it, my Vans covering my feet and my Tommy Hilfiger wrapped around my left wrist. I jumped off the stairs and walked up to the door. I looked at my watch and it was 7 already.

"Mum?" I called out. No one answered. I took my iPhone out of my jeans' pocket and dialled her number. She picked it up after a few minutes and I spoke into my iPhone, "Hey, mum, I'm going out for pizza with Ashwini and the others, okay?" She spoke back, "Okay. Get back home before 10." I nodded my head and said, "Will do. See ya." I hung up and shoved my iPhone back into my pocket. I opened the main door and walked out of the house, shutting the door behind me. I looked up at the dark sky and said to myself, "Wow, it's dark. So, should I take my bike? Yeah." I walked to the garage, took the bike off its stand and rode away from our property, pedalling down to Dominos', which was on the corner of the next block.

I put my bike on stand and walked into Dominos', where I saw Dhruv sitting on one of the tables in the far left corner, flipping his Motorola open and close. I smirked and looked around the place, which was pretty empty. I walked up to Dex's table and sat down in front of him.

"Where's everyone else?" I asked as Dhruv looked up at me as I took my seat.

He smiled and replied, "Oh hey. Lakshita has tuitions. Naaz, I don't know. Ashwini, I thought you'd know." I leaned a little forward, folding my arms against the table and said, "Or maybe we're just early." He nodded his head slowly and replied, "That's another possibility." I chuckled and question, "How did your mother allow Lakshita to go out when she has her exam in another day or two?"

"Mum says Lakshita could do with some break. She says that Lakshita's brain can't take too much of math."

"Whose brain can take too much of math, anyway?"

I chuckled and scratched my cheek as my other arm still rested on the table. Dhruv acted like a smartass and said, stating the obvious, "Uh, hello. You're talking to a math-wiz here!" I shook my head and then patted his hand, which rested on the table with his Motorola in between.

"One more reason why I hate you," I said with a quiet smile. He inhaled and exhaled loudly, rolling his eyes. "Anyway," I said, trying not to laugh at Dhruv's expressions. "I heard it's the All You Can Eat Buffet today." Dhruv narrowed his eyes and asked all confused, "No, no, that's a Pizza Hut thing." I flicked my hair back and replied, "It doesn't matter. It's food! Anything related to food makes me happy." He nodded his head and laughed lightly, "Alright then." I rocked my legs slowly and impatiently because I could not stand the smell of pizza any longer. I sighed a little and then looked at the door and saw Naaz and Ashwini walk in, talking to each other like they were debating, which was weird because Ashwini wasn't much of a debater. Naaz was, though. I smiled as they walked in.

"Finally!" I exclaimed as I looked at Dhruv and I clapped excitedly. He stifled a laugh. Ashwini and Naaz walked over to our table and Naaz sat next to me while Ashwini sat on the chair at the width of the table. I looked at Ashwini and asked a little angrily, "What the hell took you so long?" She raised her eyebrows and replied, taking the menu-card from the centre of the table, "I'm sorry, you said 8, as far as I remember." I sighed and took the menu-card away from her, "There is no specific time for pizza. Pizza can be eaten anytime, so shut up, please. You're bringing this place's IQ down." Dhruv and Naaz laughed as I looked at the menu-card and Ashwini's jaw dropped. Naaz covered her mouth and continued laughing silently. Dhruv stopped laughing and asked, "That's from Sherlock, isn't it?" I nodded my head as I flipped through the thick pages of the blue and red menu-card. Ashwini pouted and folded her arms. The waitress came and stood there and said, "Good evening, kids. My name is Kristine and I will be your waitress this evening." I smiled and said, "Oh good. Okay, Kristine, how about you get us five cokes, and two plates of stuffed Garlic Bread, and let's get a large farmhouse pizza, and two plates of chicken tacos." She nodded her head and wrote the order down on her script pad. Ashwini interrupted and said, "Make that four cokes and one diet coke." Naaz, Dhruv and I looked at her and Naaz said, sarcastically, "Wow. Diet coke and pizza – there are no calories at all." Kristine laughed and so did I. Naaz continued, "I'll have a Mexican green-wave pizza, small." She nodded her head, looked at Ashwini and asked, "And you, miss?" Ashwini looked back at her and replied, "Ah, the regular – I'll have a fresh green salad." Kristine then looked at Dhruv, "And you, sir?" Dhruv smiled and replied as he looked at me, "Nikita just ordered for me. Chicken tacos." Kristine smiled back and nodded her head and took the menu cards from us and said, "Okay – four cokes, one diet coke, two plates of stuffed garlic bread, a large farmhouse pizza, two plates chicken tacos, one small Mexican green-wave pizza and a fresh green salad. Your order will be ready in 20-25 minutes. Apologies in advance if there's any delay. Thank you." She walked away as I sighed. Ashwini smiled and put her elbows on the table and said, "This feels so nice. Just five, when Lex gets here, of us best friends dining together." I smiled and replied, "Yeah, it is good for a change after all the hurricanes that have struck me."

Ashwini looked at me lovingly and said in a sweet voice, "No hurricanes, just lessons." She smiled. I looked at her and replied promptly, "Yeah, why don't you scoff your preaching down your throat?" Her jaw dropped slightly and she averted her gaze after saying, "So it's okay when Nikita Achanta preaches but not okay when Ashwini Kamboj does."

I laughed slightly and leaned back into my chair. "It's one of the few privileges I have around you."

I stared up at the ceiling and then heard Dhruv say, "And here comes my sister." I looked at him and then turned around in my chair and smiled as I saw Lakshita walk in with her bag hanging on her shoulders.

"Hey, you guys," she said with exhaustion in her voice as she walked up to us. She went over and sat next to Dhruv. She removed her bag from her shoulders and gently dropped it to the floor under the table.

"You took your time," I said, turning towards her and leaning back into my chair. She sighed, rolling her eyes and replied, "You have no idea how tough this year's math is." I raised my right eyebrow and leaned forward, bringing my arms on the table, and said, "Been there, done that, darling." She shrugged her shoulders and looked around the table, her eyes searching for a menu-card. She said a little angrily, "Where is the damn menu-card? I am starving." Ashwini looked at her and replied politely, "We already ordered." Lakshita nodded and then smiled slightly, looking here and there. I sighed deeply and then looked at Naaz as she spoke, "Let's talk about something. Nikita!" She turned towards me, one arm of hers on the table, and continued, "What's your favourite TV series?" I narrowed my eyes slightly, searching for the perfect answer, I then answered, "Castle, Big Bang Theory, Sherlock, yeah." Ashwini then interrupted by saying, "Sherlock comes on BBC." I looked at her and she continued, "We don't get BBC in India, according to me."

"Yeah, then again, what is the internet for?"

"I saw one of your posts on your admin page, about Johnlock, whatever. That's Sherlock and...?"

"That is Sherlock and John's ship name. You know, pairing."

"Those two are together?"

"Uh, no. That'd be weird. But the Sherlock fandom, including me, likes to think of them as one. As a ship."

"Ah. And then there's MorMor, I don't even have a clue what that is."

"That is Jim Moriarty and Sebastian Moran, his right-hand man."

"Wow, that's— "

"No, trust me, you do not want to ship MorMor. I can't ship MorMor. I just can't picture them together, that's just – no."

"But, Nikita, a guy liking another guy is totally— "

I snapped out of my patience and said a little angrily and with a little haste in my voice, "Yes, I get it that it's really weird for you and these three but it's not weird for me," Ashwini jumped back into her chair slightly. I continued, "When you're a part of way too many fandoms, you get used to stuff like this." She rose her hands up in defence and said meekly, "Yeah, alright, I-I get it." I reclined back into my chair and gently tapped my fingers on the table's surface. I could hear Naaz stifling a laugh. I chuckled slightly. Naaz then asked, "But Sherlock and John are companions, right? Like, a team?" I nodded my head slightly and then replied, "Yes, they are the most amazing duo ever, just like Beckett and Castle from Castle. And besides," I turned my eyes to Ashwini as she scrolled through the messages on her phone, I continued with a slight smile, "Every Holmes must have his Watson. And Ash is my Watson." Ashwini looked up at me as I said that. I then said, "But in this case, every Moriarty must have his Moran, so Ash is my Moran while I'm Moriarty." She crossed her eyebrows and asked, clueless as she seemed, "What are you even saying?" I laughed under my breath and answered, "And this is why sometimes I pity that you don't read books or watch BBC." She shoved her phone back into her jeans' pocket and asked again, "And why should I even watch BBC?"

I shook my head slightly and answered like a true fangirl, "BBC: Because Benedict Cumberbatch."

She smirked slightly, sighed and said, looking away, "Yeah, I'll pass."

sixteen.

Our order arrived a few minutes later. Kristine put down all that we'd ordered on our table and said with a smile, "Please, enjoy." She then walked off and all of us started eating. I took a piece of the stuffed garlic bread and took a bite after dipping it in the jalapeno dipping. After finishing our side orders, each of us picked up a slice of pizza each and as Ashwini was about to take a huge bite, I stopped her and said, "No, wait, wait, wait." She looked at me and brought the slice of pizza away from her mouth. I sighed a little happily and then said, bringing my slice a little into the air like a toast, "Here's a pizza toast," All four of them raised their slices as well and I continued, "A toast to friendship, and to pizza." All of us laughed and then bumped our slices lightly against each other's and then took a bite. We all feasted happily on our pizzas and side orders.

After a few minutes, as Naaz was munching on her second slice of pizza, I looked at her and saw a little cheese trail down the corner of her lip. "Hey, Naaz?" I held my glass of coke in my hand. She turned her head towards me while still munching on her pizza. I continued, "You've got a little cheese down your lip."

I reached my free hand forward and used my index finger to wipe away the melted cheese.

"Here." I smiled slightly and then licked my cheese-dipped finger. Naaz looked at me all weird and asked, "Um, a little gross, why did you just do that?" I licked the tip of my finger and replied blandly, "Uh, because cheese." She laughed lightly and then took another bite of her pizza slice. I looked at Lakshita as she stared at her slice of pizza with love and affection. She munched quietly and then said, "You know what, eating pizza inspires me to do greater things in life." All four of us looked at her and she continued, still staring at the slice, "For example, eating more pizza." All of us laughed again and she laughed as well, taking a huge bite of her slice. I put my glass of coke down and picked up one of the remaining two chicken tacos. I took a small bite of it, trying not to let the cheese escape from the other opening of the taco.

Ashwini looked at me and asked, "I thought you were vegetarian." I nodded my head, munching on the deliciousness of the taco, and replied, "Yeah, but then," I swallowed. "I started to think logically. Like, why the hell did we, humans, fight to the top of the food chain? To munch on vegetables and green stuff? I don't think so." Dhruv chuckled and licked the cheese off his shirt's sleeve, he said, "Does that mean you don't love animals anymore?" I turned my head towards him and then said defensively, "Now that is completely untrue. I love animals more than most of the human population. And I always will. But then again, this poor chicken," I sighed as I looked at the taco in my hand, "My brother said this poor chicken was meant to die, so be it." I shrugged my shoulders slightly and took a bite of my taco. Ashwini smiled slightly and then got back to munching on her slice of pizza.

"On another note," I said. "Cillian Murphy is a vegetarian." Ashwini cocked up a smile and asked, "So are you planning on turning back into a vegetarian, Miss Obsessed?"

I glared at her and replied unpleasantly, "Eat your pizza before I scoff it down your shirt."

seventeen.

We finished our 'dinner' and Kristine brought the bill.

"Ah," I said smiling, taking the bill-jacket from her. I narrowed my eyes slightly as I looked at the bill after opening the jacket, and then said in an opposite tone, "Oh."

Ashwini looked at me and then tried to look at the bill, she asked, "How much is it?" I reached for my wallet in my jeans' hip pocket and said, taking it out, "Hush. This is my treat, remember?" She nodded her head and retracted back into her chair. I took out three notes of five hundred each and shoved them into the bill-jacket and shut it close, handing it back to Kristine, I smiled and thanked her as she walked away. I shoved my wallet back into my jeans' pocket and then stood up, all four of them standing as well. Lakshita hung her bag on her shoulder and we all walked out of the Dominos' building. I hopped onto my bike, Dhruv and Lakshita on their own aviators and Ashwini sat onto her activa, Naaz sitting behind her.

"Alright then," I said as I gripped my bike's handlebars. "See you guys whenever then?"

Dhruv nodded his head, turning his aviator on and turning it to drive out of the 'parking lot'. He said with a smile, "Whenever it is then." I smiled and turned my bike around as well. All of us bid goodbye to each other and I pedalled back home.

It was almost 10 as I put my bike back on its stand in the parking lot. I walked up to the main door and rang the bell. I waited for a moment and then dad opened the door.

"Hey," he said with a smile. I smiled back and walked in, and replied, "Hello there." He shut the door behind us and we walked to the lobby and my smile sort of faded away when I saw Samira sitting on the couch and talking to mum. I chuckled slightly and said, "Hi, Samira." She turned around, flicking her long brown curly hair back. She passed me a shark-like grin, then got up and walked over to me. She exclaimed, "Hey, Nikita!" She wrapped her arms around me and hugged me tightly, almost squeezing me. I refrained slightly but then hugged her back as I rolled my eyes and replied, "Hi." She let go off me and ran her eyes over me and then said, observantly, "Wow. Been too long. You look good, kid." I smiled forcefully and replied, "Yeah, don't call me 'kid'." She looked at me and then let out a laugh and then pressed her pouty lips together, "I can see that you're a proper teen now." I raised my eyebrows and said, "Uh, yeah. Kind of. But still immature, don't worry." She laughed again and I thought to myself, "Jesus, she hasn't let go of her laughing habit still. Who even does that now?" I then snapped out of it and heard her say, "Wow. You've changed."

"Yeah, I'm a freaking transformer."

I rolled my eyes and looked over at my mum, who sat there on the black couch. I smiled slightly and said, "I'll be upstairs, Ma. I'm really sleepy. G'night, people." I was about to walk upstairs to my room but stopped when I heard mum say, "Samira's sharing your room with you for the time she's here." I turned around on my heels and said, smiling mockingly, "Lovely. Come on, Samira." I sighed slightly and continued, "I'll show you my little piece of heaven." I turned around and walked up the stairs and then opened the door and turned on the lights by pressing the switch with the Harry Potter spell 'Lumos' written on the bottom and 'Nox' on the bottom. I walked in and leaned against my wooden cabinet. Samira walked in and put her suitcase to the side.

"Wow," she said, awestruck as she took a look around my room. She saw the Garfield posters up on my study table's cabinets. She then looked around and walked forward, looking up at the wall next to my bed, where hung a framed photograph of Omar Abdullah with his autograph in the upper right corner, and a framed photograph of Mini ma'am and me from November 2012. In the middle of those two hung a string with NASA Space Centre written and Pirates of the Caribbean badges all over it, including my class 7th Monitor badge, class 8th Prefect badge and class 10th Vice Captain badge. She smiled slightly and then turned around to look at me.

"This is just...amazing," she said. I smiled widely and scratched my cheek and saw Samira walk up to the opposite wall. Now, this wall was very special and dear to me. In the centre was a green notice-board with quotes on printed paper and a drawing that Naaz made for me at the end of my class 9th. Around the notice-board, I had pasted and put up black and white photo printouts of my favourite celebrities. I walked up to her and stood next to her, admiring the wall. I folded my arms and gazed at all the photographs. Photos of:

- Johnny Depp: My first love.
- Cillian Murphy: My uncontrollable obsession and the guy I'd happily marry.
- Ben Whishaw: The cutest guy ever.
- Andrew Scott: Irish, need I say more?
- Tom Hiddleston: The one with the awesome cheekbones and eyes.
- George Harrison and The Beatles: My favourite of The Beatles, and also, my favourite band.
- Liv Tyler: My girl-crush. Who can resist that lady? Totally adorable.
- Stana Katic: Detective Kate Beckett, badass, enough said.
- James McAvoy: Drop-dead gorgeous.
- Tom Cruise: God made him perfect. Don't look at that smile; you'll be dead in seconds.
- Billie Joe Armstrong: Sure this man is 41? Looks pretty young to me. One word: legendary.

Samira smiled and said to me, "Your room's so creative and beautiful." I smiled back and replied, pointing to the wall, "This is my fangirl wall. It means a lot to me. I put in a lot of effort to get this up." She nodded her head and then yawned.

"You must be tired," I looked at her as she closed her mouth after nodding her head once.

"Quite," she replied. I nodded my head and said in my cold voice,

"Let's get you tucked in. I'll take you for coffee tomorrow. Come on."

She smiled.

eighteen.

Next morning, I stretched my body and turned to the other side on my single bed. I snuggled into the pillow and then opened my eyes and sat up. I ran a hand through my hair and then picked up my iPhone from the bedside table. I unlocked it and went through the notifications.

I sighed as I noticed the time, 12:45 pm.

I clicked the sleep button on the top of the iPhone and put it back on the bedside and got out of my bed. I looked over and noticed that Samira wasn't in bed - the comfy mattress on the floor. I slipped my feet into my fuzzy slippers and picked up my specs from the bedside and put them on. I walked down to the lobby sleepily. Samira was sitting on the table and reading the newspaper.

"Good morning," I said as I stepped down from the last step. She looked at me and smiled, "Lovely morning, today." I nodded my head and yawned, walking into the kitchen to make some coffee for myself. I was about to turn on the coffeemaker but stopped as I heard Samira shout, "No, don't!" I jumped in my slippers and turned around almost instantly,

"What? What happened?" I asked. She shook her head and said, "Oh, nothing. We're going out for coffee, right?" My shoulders drooped and I asked, yet again, "What? Right now?" She stood up from her chair and nodded her head quickly, she answered, "Yes, why not." I sighed deeply and walked out of the kitchen and stood on the first step of the stairs. I said, "Give me half an hour to get ready." She smiled and replied excitedly, "Of course!" I walked up the stairs and went to my room to get ready. I shut the door behind me and leaned against it for a moment.

I looked around and then said to myself, "She stopped me from making a cup of coffee for myself." I bit my lower lip and continued, "I will murder her in her sleep." Then I shook my head and walked to the bathroom to get ready for the day.

After half an hour, I walked downstairs. I wore my favourite blue jeans, my Beatles T-shirt, my Vans, a Tommy Hilfiger watch wrapped around my wrist and my titanium ring, with a wolf carved in it, slipped onto my left hand's index finger. I jumped off from the second-last step and looked at Samira, still sitting at the table.

"Ready to go?" I asked, shoving my hands into my jeans' pockets. She looked at me and then got up, nodded her head and replied, "Ready." I smirked and shouted out, "Ma?" I walked to her room and peeped in.

"We're going for coffee," I said. She nodded her head as she arranged the pile of clothes.

She smiled and replied, "Be nice."

"I'm always nice."

"Really now?"

"Well. Sometimes."

"Uh-huh."

"Occasionally."

"Bingo!"

"Fine, I'll be nice. Bye."

She chuckled as I turned around and walked up to the main door. I opened it and said to Samira who was standing behind me with her purse in her hand, "Let's go." She smiled and walked behind me as I walked out of the house. I hopped onto my bike and took it off its stand. Samira stood next to me as I gripped the handlebars. I looked at her and asked with a blank expression, "What?" She looked at the pillion-like seat behind me and replied, "So I'll hop on then." She was about to sit behind but I jerked my bike to the other side and said frantically, "No, no, no, no, no! That's not the way it works around here, missy."

"So you're going to ride your bike, how am I supposed to travel?"

"On foot. Be eco-friendly, honey."

"But... okay, how far is this place?"

"Baker's Lounge, six minutes walk on foot."

"What the--?"

"Come on now, chop-chop."

She sighed as I turned my bike around and pedalled slowly out of the parking lot and away from home.

nineteen.

We reached this cafeteria called Baker's Lounge which was a few minutes away from my place. Samira and I walked in after I put my bike on its stand outside the building. We walked further into the building and sat on a table in front of the pasta counter. I ran my hand through my slightly wet hair and then looked at Samira as she folded her arms against the table. She smirked and said, "So I hear you're pretty much anti-social." I narrowed my gaze and asked startled, "Asocial. But who told you that? H-how do you know?" She laughed lightly and replied, "Your mum told me when I came yesterday." I managed to force a smile. I said, "Ah. My mum gave it away, okay."

"Why?"

"Why, what?"

"Why are you anti-social? You look like one of those persons who get along with people very well."

"Asocial. And no. No need to be modest. I do not."

"Yes, you do. And you know what? I'll teach you how to socialise!"

I let out a laugh almost instantly and then said, "You can't teach me something god failed to do." She grinned cockily and replied, "We'll see about that. I'll go order coffee." She was about to get up, but I stood up before her and pushed her down gently into her seat by her shoulders.

"No," I protested. "I'll go. I don't like people ordering coffee for me."

She nodded and then admired her crimson red nails. I walked up to the ordering counter and placed an order for one large Irish coffee with whipped cream and one medium cappuccino. I walked back to the table and sat on my chair.

I sighed slightly and then looked at Samira and asked out of curiosity, "How does this teach-Nikita-to-socialize-thing work, anyway?" She looked at me with lit up eyes and replied, "Oh! It's simple. Give me your hand." I looked at her and then looked at my hands lying on the table. I shook my head and said, coldly, "I don't like to be touched." She stifled a chuckle and replied, "Sorry." She reached her hand out and lightly patted my right hand. I said, trying not to sound rude or unpleasant, "That includes hugging, tapping me on the shoulder and patting my hands."

"What do you do on holidays?" She asked as she pulled her hand back.

"I spend all day in my bed when I'm home – I'm too sad to do anything but lay there."

"Friends?"

"Most of my friends don't seem to care about me; I only have a limited number of friends. I don't like people invading my personal space."

"Do you care about the small bunch of friends you have?"

"Of course, I do. I hate people, it's why I don't have many friends, but if there's one person I care about who's my age, that's my best friend, Dhruv, even though he's a jackass."

"How is he different from others?"

"He hasn't given up on me. Even after all arguments, misunderstandings, petty little fights – strangely enough, he hasn't given up on me. Not yet."

"Wow. He sounds like a great person."

"He's one of those people I like. Someone whose existence I appreciate." I chuckled.

"That's really cute."

"Cute? If you say so."

"Is he your boyfriend?"

"Dhruv?" I laughed a little. "No! No, I am single – Guys don't understand me and neither do they like me. My obsessions are way too great to handle."

"I noticed your room's a mess."

"I'm a mess. I'm a catastrophe, in some people's words. I don't like to clean my room. The messiness is my organization."

"Right. Okay. I got you."

She nodded her head lightly and I then said, breaking the silence, "You make me feel like shit, you realise that?" She looked at me and tried saying, "I—" I chuckled lightly and continued, interrupting her before she could even start her sentence, "I already feel that way." She looked at me; I could see a little pity in her eyes. I smirked and said, "Don't pity me. The last thing I want is to see pity in someone's eyes for me." She shook her head and averted her gaze and exclaimed,

"Oh look!" She smiled and then looked at me, "The waiter's coming over with our coffee." I smiled slightly and the waiter walked up to us and placed our cups on the table. I smiled at him and pulled my cup closer to myself as he walked away. Samira widened her eyes slightly and asked, "What did you order for yourself? That looks amazing." I smiled and used my finger to pull off some of the dripping whipped cream. I licked my finger and said, "Irish coffee with whipped cream. I just love Irish stuff." She brought her cup close to her lips and asked, "And what does that stuff include?" I took a sip of my coffee and answered, "Ireland. Irish. Irish scenery, Irish coffee, Irish accent, Irish—" Before I could complete the sentence, Samira said, "Irish men?" I looked at her, once again, with narrowed eyes, and questioned, "Dude, what?"

She laughed and answered, "Andrew Scott is Irish? And so is that Cillian guy. Come on. I saw your fangirl wall." She winked at me and took another sip of her coffee.

I forced a smile and looked away, licking a little of the whipped cream.

twenty.

Samira and I walked inside my house through the door. She walked up the stairs and said, "I'm going to go get fresh." I nodded and she plodded up the stairs. I watched her enter my room. I suddenly turned around and walked to my mother's room. I drifted through the door and said frantically, "Ma!" She was sitting on the rocking chair and reading 'Anastasia,' the book I had gifted her for her 50th birthday. She looked up at me and asked, "Yes?" I stood in front of her and replied, placing my hand on my chest, "I am so not good at socialising." She laughed lightly and said as she removed her specs, "Oh, I know that. But I'm pretty sure you were nice to her." I looked up at the ceiling and said, "Well, I wasn't rude or mean to her either. I mean, as far as I think. Don't worry. She's all smiling and happy." She smiled quietly and said, "There's this one thing I like about you, Nikita."

"And what might that be, mother?"

"Even if you despise a person, no matter how much, you're always willing to cope up with them if a loved one asks you to."

"That's-that's not true."

"You wouldn't have been nice to Samira if I hadn't asked you to."

"Well, I—"

"Now do you agree with that or not?"

I sighed in defeat and replied as I bit the inside of my right cheek, "I agree with that. That makes me so vulnerable. So weak."

My mum shook her head and replied, "Not vulnerable. It's not a weakness." I looked at her. She continued and said ever so lovingly, "It's a strength."

I smiled back at her and said, backing off slowly, "I'll hold on to that." She nodded her head and smiled one last time, and then put her specs back on and got back to reading the book.

As Dhruv would say, quoting John Green, "For me, the hero's journey is not the voyage from weakness to strength. The true hero's journey is the voyage from strength to weakness."

part two.

one.

Samira left a day before the date of my farewell. And the farewell arrived.

It was 5 in the evening as I tied the laces on my Nike dunks. I stood up from my bed and stretched my feet inside my shoes. I wore my favourite blue jeans, my Pink Floyd shirt with the Dark Side of the Moon symbol printed on it, a black-checked white over-shirt and as always, my Tommy Hilfiger watch and titanium ring. I picked up my iPhone from the table and shoved it into my jeans' pocket and hung my side-bag over my right shoulder. I then walked up to the corner of my Fangirl Wall and picked up my acoustic guitar as it rested in its black velvet case. I then walked up to the door and shut off the lights and then hurried downstairs. Mum stood there with a cup of tea in one hand and her phone in the other.

"I'll be off then, Ma," I said as I stepped down from the last step of the staircase.

"So soon?" she asked.

"Well, yes. I don't want Ashwini, the host, to be mad at me."

"Okay. Taking your camera?"

"Ma, I have an iPhone 4. What do I need a camera for?"

"Photographs."

"With an 8-megapixel built-in camera, this iPhone is all I'll ever need to survive on a deserted island."

She laughed lightly and I smiled.

"Take care, then," She said. "And have fun."

I nodded my head and walked up to the door and replied, "Will do, ma." I walked out, shutting the door behind me. I opened the gate and saw Lakshita there, sitting on her aviator. She said with a smile, "Hey." I smiled and walked up to her as I locked the gate behind me.

"Ready?" I asked. She nodded her head and gestured to the seat behind her. I climbed on, holding my guitar to the right side, I said, "Let's go, then." We rode away off the property.

Lakshita parked her aviator outside the school's front gate and we got off. She pulled down her shirt and I looked at her, toe to head. She wore low-heels, her blue skinny jeans, a long top with flowers printed on it and a few bracelets on both her wrists. She had kept her hair open and wore a hair-band. I smiled and passed her a compliment, "You look pretty." She chuckled and replied, "Thanks. Dhruv said I look hideous." I gripped my guitar's case handle a little tighter and asked, "Doesn't he say that to every girl he knows?" She looked at me all cockily and said, "A hundred bucks on line if he doesn't say you look stunning." I pulled on a blank expression and replied, "I look like I look every day."

She nodded. "He's my brother. You think I don't know him?"

"Uh—"

"Nikita. Dude."

"Oh, right. He has a crush on me. I keep forgetting that."

"I'll text you every day from now on, reminding you that my petty jackass-of-a-brother likes you."

"No, thank you. I'll keep that in mind."

She chuckled as the two of us walked through the gate and to the main ground where the event was being held.

"Oh, Lakshita," I stopped and said as we were about to step into the tent. She looked at me and asked, "Yeah?" I pointed to the stage and replied, "I'm gonna go backstage. I know my performance is last but I have to check if they have a drummer." She nodded her head and walked into the pink tent. I turned around and walked to the stage from the side. I walked along an array of gladiolas set in numerous of earthen pots and vases. I smiled a little as I saw the various colours as my feet carried me backstage with my guitar case in one hand. I went up the stairs to backstage.

I saw Ashwini standing there with files in her hands. She wore a long black frock-like dress with slight high-heels, black as well. I saw her nervously tap her feet on the ground as she went through the files. I smirked and walked up to her.

"Nervous?" I asked as I approached her, making my way through the performing crowd, trying not to bump my guitar case against anyone. She looked at me and sighed, "You have no idea how much." I stood next to her and she continued, "I'm terrified. What if I screw this up?" I wrapped an arm around her shoulder and replied, "You won't. Trust me."

She looked into my eyes and said, anxious as she was, "I thought... by this time... you would have given up on me."

I passed her a comforting and reassuring smile, "Never."

She smiled back at me and looked back at the files. I took my arm back and asked, "So do you have a drummer for me?" She bit her lower lip and shut her eyes. I chuckled unpleasantly and continued, "I'll take that as a no." She turned on her tiptoes and said to me, guilt in her voice, "I'm sorry. I'm so sorry. I couldn't find anyone." I frowned but didn't say anything. She looked at me with sorrowful eyes and then said, almost immediately, "I'll find you one. I promise." I stood up the guitar case against my body, leaned against it and asked, "Really? Where, in this crowd of bloodsuckers, are you going to find me a drummer who knows songs by Imagine Dragons? Huh?" Ashwini sighed slightly and looked down. I shook my head and continued, sighing deeply, "It's alright. I'll figure something out." She looked up at me and I passed her a reassuring smile. She half-smiled and questioned, "You want to keep your guitar and backpack somewhere safe?" I looked at my guitar and then back at her, "Yes, that'd be nice." She pointed to a few lockers behind her and said, "There. My locker number's 8. Just shove your bag in there and hand your guitar over to me. They'll be safe." I looked all confused and asked her out of surprise, "Since when did our school authorities get lockers?" She chuckled and licked her lips and answered, "Just for events like these. Here." She reached into her outfit's pocket and took out a small golden key and handed it over to me. I took it from her and she said, "Return the key to me once you put your bag into the locker and yes, give me your guitar." She reached her hand out and I handed my guitar in its velvet case carefully. She took it from me and smiled, then walked away with my guitar. I tossed the key lightly into the air and then caught it back in my hand. I walked up to the green lockers and searched for #8. I ran my eyes through the locker numbers and then found the one I was looking for. But it was blocked by a girl in a weird purple dress and a guy in a black mime costume, who were hugging in front of my locker. I rolled my eyes and thought to myself, "Of course. Hug in front of my locker. I've got all day for this." The two of them then exchanged smiles and walked away. I let out a sigh of relief and then thought to myself, again, "I'm so glad they didn't exchange saliva." I walked up to the locker and inserted the key into the little metallic lock. I turned the key to the right side twice and it opened up with a click. I took off the lock and opened the locker's door by the handle. I shoved the lock along with the key into my jeans' right hip pocket. I then took off my side bag and gently placed it into the locker. I shut the locker's door and put the lock back in its place and turned the key to the left side once and locked up the locker. I walked away and my eyes searched for Ashwini everywhere. I saw her standing at the wooden dais, going through a file. I made my way through the small crowd of performers by gently pushing them out of the way. I walked up to her and chucked the key on the dais. She heard the clack and looked at the key and then at me, as I looked at the curtains that covered the stage. She smirked and took the key, putting it back into her outfit's pocket. I looked at her and narrowed my eyes.

I looked around and then asked, "Where's my guitar?" She pointed under the dais' base, still looking at a piece of paper. I kept both my hands on the dais and leaned my head forward to see my guitar, resting peacefully in its case in a hollow space under the dais. I looked at her and said with a smile, "Lovely." She smiled back and I continued, retracting back, "Catch you later. Do well. Don't screw this up." She laughed as she looked at me, and replied, "I won't screw this up. Promise." I smiled and walked away, making my way down the platform from the stairs I walked up from and then walked into the crowd of 10th graders, 9th graders and teachers.

I sighed happily and said to myself, "It's Showtime."

two.

I walked casually through the crowd, meeting and greeting everyone present there, forcing smiles, etcetera, etcetera, etcetera – the usual social criteria. I then looked around and saw Lakshita talking to Naaz. I smiled and walked up to them.

"Hey, guys," I said with a pleasant smile. I then looked at Naaz, from heel to head. She wore a pair of blue ragged jeans, a Madame top, her hair made up into a bun, and lots of groovy bangles around both her wrists. Lakshita looked at me and replied with a smile, "Oh, here." She handed me a glass containing a pinkish-red liquid. I took it from her and took a sip. I narrowed my eyes slightly and asked, "What is that?" She took the glass back from me and replied, chuckling, "That's punch." I looked at her with raised eyebrows, "Punch? Our school's trying all sorts of new things, huh?" She nodded her head a couple of times. I then looked over at Naaz who was looking elsewhere. I snapped my right hand's fingers in front of her face and asked, "Still in there?" She pushed my hand away and gave me a disgusted look. I looked at Lakshita and Lakshita looked at me. The two of us leaned our heads close and I asked her in a whisper, "What's happening here?" She whispered back,

"She was behaving alright before you showed up." The two of us pulled our heads back. I adjusted my glasses and asked Naaz, "Did I do something wrong?" Naaz laughed slightly, but not a laughter of joy. She then replied, shaking both her fists, "Oh, where do I even begin!" I raised my left eyebrow and suppressed the right one. She then continued, "I called you last week." I gulped and replied a little nervously, "Yeah, you did. I wasn't in town, actually. I was spending quality time with my brother in Chandigarh." She folded both her arms and said angrily, "It was my brother's birthday. And since you didn't pick up your phone, you missed the party."

I chuckled. "So you're mad at me because I didn't show up for your brother's birthday party?"

"We could have had some 'us' time."

"My brother and I needed some 'us' time, too. I was out and—"

"It's like you don't have time for me anymore."

"Dude." I scratched my right cheek. "Where the hell is this coming from?"

"From where the truth comes."

"That's not the truth."

"It's like I'm always in your way and you don't want anything to do with me." She sounded tired. Of me.

"That's just preposterous."

"Yeah, put it away with a stupid word," she said as she turned around and walked away.

I got angry as well and shouted from behind, a mere voice couldn't stop her because of the music playing in the background, "Hey, listen!" She turned around and gave me a stern look. I shook my head slightly and let out a deep sigh. I continued, "Why am I the one who's always packing up my stuff?" She shrugged her shoulders and then turned around, walking away as I felt displeasure in her movements. I sighed and then looked at Lakshita. She wrapped an arm around my shoulder and whispered, taking a sip of her punch, "She'll come to. I know she will."

I nodded my head and as she was about to take another sip, I took the glass from her hand and brought it near my lips, "And till she doesn't, I have you and this glass of punch to go."

The two of us laughed together.

three.

Lakshita and I walked around the crowd, expressing our regards and gratitude for all our teachers who taught us, from grade 1st to grade 10th. We were speaking to one of our 8th grade teachers. I got sucked out of the conversation by my boredom and looked around the place and saw Mini ma'am standing there, talking to Dhruv. She wore a black sari with a golden border. She had kept her dark brown hair open. She wore her smile and beautiful brown eyes. She looked stunning. The ghost of a smile tugged at my lips. Then I got dragged away as I heard Lakshita say, "Eh, Nikita?" I looked at her as she and the teacher wore smiles on their faces. I asked, "What?" Lakshita wore off the smile and said, "That Mrs. Finch is a great teacher. Don't you agree?" I nodded my head and said with a smile covering my lips, "She is. The only reason I'm good at maths is because of her." Mrs. Finch smiled and replied, "I'm flattered, child." I nodded my head and then said, "If you'll excuse me. Mrs Finch. Lakshita." The two of them nodded their heads and I walked away and up to Mini ma'am and Dhruv.

I pulled on my charming smile and said, "Hello, beautiful people." The two of them turned towards me and smiled.

"Hi," said Mini ma'am with her great smile. I looked at her, "Well, hello, beautiful and..." I then shifted my gaze to Dhruv and continued, "...jackass." Mini ma'am chuckled.

Dhruv wore his black jeans, a black and white collar-shirt, sleeves rolled up his forearms. He looked pretty good, though. His sharp cheekbones looked more prominent than ever and his black eyes went perfectly with his thin eyebrows. He had a positively evil look on his face. One I positively liked.

He said, shoving his hands into his jeans' pockets, "Ah, Nikita. Always so mature." I passed him a smug grin and then felt it change into a smile, as Mini ma'am said, immediately after Dhruv completed his sentence, "Always so charming." I chuckled and said to Dhruv, "You heard the lady." He nodded his head and gave me a thumbs up. He then looked at me and said, I could feel him at a loss of words, "You look stunning today."

I didn't know what to say. "Dude, I look like I look every day."

"Yes, but every day, you don't give me a chance to compliment you. You break it down by calling me a 'jackass'."

"Whoever said I would let you compliment me today?"

"Because... this might be the last social gathering you and I attend together."

A weird silence pulled me away as the fact that I was leaving in a few months struck me. I smiled slightly, but a true smile, and said, "Thanks, Dex. Compliment duly noted." He smiled at me and sighed happily. I heard Mini ma'am say, "I'll leave you kids to it then." She turned around to leave. I looked at her and said frantically, my hands reaching out for her, "No, no, no, no, no." I then looked at Dhruv and whispered to him, faking my anger, "Jackass." He laughed lightly and used his right index and middle fingers to grab my nose lightly. I scrunched my nose and smiled and so did he. I loved it. But I soon pushed his hand away, stuck my tongue out at him and walked up to Mini ma'am. She turned around and looked at me. I scratched my forehead and said, at a loss of words as I was, "You look, uh…" I chuckled lightly. She moved a little closer and said with a grin, "Go ahead. I won't bite." I averted my gaze as she looked into my eyes and I replied, "Yes, because the first thing I'd like to say to you before complimenting is, 'Oh my god, don't turn me into a zombie by biting me,' right?" She laughed lightly, placing her hand, nails painted crimson red, in front of her lips. I looked at her and laughed along.

"Glad that made you laugh," I said.

"You always make me laugh."

"I know, because I'm always so mature," I said in a tone similar to Dhruv's.

"Anyway, you were saying?"

"What was I saying?"

She bit the corner of her lower lip and said, "You are impossible, you are." I nodded my head and replied,

"That I am. Can't help it. My apologies." She grinned and looked away, folding her arms. I smiled slightly and said in a low pitch, my voice not so cold, "You look beautiful." She looked at me as I completed the sentence. I raised up my shoulders slightly and then dropped them back, shoving my hands into my jeans' pockets, "I just had to put it out there." She gently held my nose by her right hand's thumb and index finger and shook my face lightly, saying playfully, "You are so predictable." She let go off my nose and smiled. I rubbed my nose with my left hand and asked, "I'm predictable?" She nodded her head in agreement. I pulled my hand back and sighed as I looked down. I looked back up at her as she said, "But yet so meticulously stupendous."

I smiled. "I'll take that as a compliment."

"I don't expect you to be offended."

She passed me a comforting smile and ran a hand through her hair.

"Cute," I said. "Very cute."

She smirked playfully and poked my nose, "I know I am."

I pushed her hand away gently and said forcefully, "For heaven's sake, stop with the poking already." Her smirk faded away and she replied in a low tone, "But you're so poke-able." I looked at her all confused and said, flicking my hair back, "I don't even think that's a word."

She shook her head, "I just made it up."

I nodded my head approvingly. "Aren't we all fun tonight!"

"Aren't we always?"

She nudged my arm playfully and winked. I smiled and raised my left fist up to my shoulder level, "We are."

She smiled back and bumped her left, as well, fist against mine, pressing her gold ring against my titanium ring.

four.

I sat on the red velvet chairs around a round table with Lakshita and three of my classmates: Jigyasa, Ria and Ashwini. I sat there, spinning the titanium ring, on my left index finger, around.

"Yeah, so if you actually think of people dying," said Jigyasa as we talked of the very random topic of bomb-blasts, "It's sad on so many levels." Lakshita gently tapped her fingers on the table and said, sorrow in her voice, "People have died." I stopped spinning my ring and looked at Lakshita and I said with a chuckle, "That's what people do." Ria gave me a puzzled look and asked, "People die every day?" I nodded my head and replied, "Yes, they do. Which is sad, if they haven't done anything to deserve it." Lakshita was about to say something but before she could, one of our teachers who taught English, Mrs Farah, walked up to our table with a mike in her hand. She placed her hand on the back of Jigyasa's chair and leaned against it. She held up the mike near her mouth and said into it with a cheeky smile covering her lips, "Good evening, everyone. I thank you all for being present here for the first ever grade 10th farewell. Now, let's not slob around and let's play some games." I looked at her and then leaned towards Lakshita and whispered to her, "Games meaning effort." Lakshita chuckled and nodded her head, "Effort, yes, but that depends on what game we're going to play." I nodded my head and retracted back into my chair. I flicked my hair back and looked at Mrs Farah. She then announced, "If all of you can move your chairs a little forward towards me, please?" I looked at Lakshita and said as I folded my arms, "Yep, that's a lot of effort involved." She laughed lightly. I looked around as all the students and teachers pulled their chairs forward and settled down.

"Hey," I turned my head to the right as I saw Ashwini sitting down on her chair. I looked at her and asked as she folded her left leg over her right knee, "How'd you manage to get off the stage?"

"It's a farewell. Just because I'm the host doesn't mean I don't get to enjoy."

"Well, you should have stayed on stage. What if you get hurt?"

"We aren't bombing battleships here, neither are we planning an assassination."

"That's disappointing."

"Oh, stop being so ruthless."

"I'm not. I'm being myself."

She chuckled and folded her arms as she looked over at Mrs Farah. Mrs Farah smiled as she looked around and then spoke into the mike, "Wonderful. Okay. Let's play a story-telling game first." I rolled my eyes and let out a groan. Lakshita nudged my shoulder lightly with her elbow and whispered, "Don't make stupid noises." I gave her a disgusted look and then looked back at Mrs Farah.

"Now…" she said as her eyes searched the crowd. She then traced her eyes along to our table and said, looking at me, into her mike, "Ah! Nikita Achanta, everyone!"

Everyone around started clapping as she completed the sentence. Lakshita was clapping too with a weird grin on her face. I pulled her hands away and asked in a whisper, "Why are you clapping?" She shook her head and exclaimed, "I don't really know!" I then looked at Mrs Farah as she said, "Now, Nikita, tell me the saddest love story you have ever encountered." I chuckled and protested, "Oh, I'm really not good with love stories. Not my thing, really." She smirked and said into the mike, spreading her other arm wide, "Are we hearing denial from the city's best orator?" I looked around as everyone made funny noises. I rolled my eyes and clenched my jaw tightly.

"Too far," I said under my breath. I then stood up from my chair and sighed. I reached my hand out to take the mike from her. She passed me a smile and gave me the mike. I took it into my right hand and nodded my head as I brought it near my lips. Keeping the mike at a distance, I spoke into it as I stood up, "Well, it all began when two babies were born in two entirely different places and time." I saw Mrs Farah sit down on one of the chairs next to Mini ma'am. I then continued, "The boy grew up to be a successful young man, with cheekbones, pretty eyes and floppy hair, who now roams around the world, showcasing his talent," I took a deep breath. "While the girl stays in the sea of faces who admire him. He doesn't know her, but she knows him; from his real name to his favourite colour. She sends him love letters, even if she's aware that he won't be able to read them and she has to pay money just to see him on screen for a few hours," I looked at Ashwini and she looked back at me, listening intently like the rest of the crowd. I continued, "That pattern goes on and on, unceasingly. The boy continues to walk in her dreams and she looks at him with pure admiration, and sadly, that's how it'll end," I sighed. "The boy will never know... just how much the girl loves him." I nodded my head and said, shoving my left hand into my jeans' pocket, "And that's about it, yeah." Everyone around started clapping. I looked over and saw Mrs Farah walking up to me. She took the mike from me and spoke into it as I sat down, "That's quite emotional and sad, Nikita."

I nodded my head rapidly and replied, "Oh, the life of a fangirl really is sad, teach." She raised her eyebrow and questioned, "What?" I shook my head, denying answering the question. I looked over at Ashwini and asked, "Was that good?" Ashwini answered with a smile as the claps faded away, "Good? That was excellent. Beautiful."

"I try my best."

"Weird how you succeed every time."

"Did Naaz, uh, applaud?"

"I looked over. She didn't."

"Ouch."

"You guys had a fight or something?"

"More like she stopped talking to me for a very, very dumb reason. You don't want to know."

"If you say so."

I looked over and saw Mini ma'am smiling. She lip-synched to me, "Good job done, kid."

I smiled and bowed my head in gratitude.

five.

Two hours later, all of us sat in our seats, our eyes fixed on the stage. The second last performance was The Z siblings' dance. The light effects at the beginning were really good. I got up from my chair and was about to make my way through the crowd when Lakshita grabbed me by my left hand and pulled me down. She asked, her voice almost cracking because of the loud music, "Where are you going?" I replied in the same pitch, "That's my queue. It's showtime." She nodded once and let go off my hand. I walked carefully, making my way through the sitting observers. I made my way through and then walked backstage.

Ashwini was standing there, tapping her fingers lightly on my guitar case as it leaned against her.

"Hey!" I said as I walked up to her. She looked at me and let out a sigh of relief, replying, "I'm so glad you're already here. Here." She handed me my guitar case and said, "Okay, Nikita, there's a problem, though."

"What?" I asked as I opened the guitar case and pulled my black Gibson Acoustic Guitar out.

"We have no drummer."

I sighed and thought for a moment. "Dhruv!" I exclaimed

"What about him?"

"I need him. Now."

"I don't think now's a good time to go on a date."

I grunted and lightly grabbed Ashwini's neck. "He's a drummer. He can play. Go get him."

She swallowed. "I'll do that. You don't worry."

She then patted my shoulder with her right hand and walked off as I let go off her neck. I put the guitar case away and carried my guitar up to the amplifiers. I took a long green wire and plugged the free end into the socket on my guitar. I sat down on a chair near the amp, placed my left hand's fingers on the brown fret-board, the other hand's around the guitar on the copper strings, and checked the tuning on my guitar.

"Perfect," I said with a quiet smile. I waited for my performance to begin. I sighed slightly as I placed my chin on my guitar. I bit my lower lip and thought of something to make it up to Naaz.

"What can I do? She's raving mad at me," I said to myself.

"I have an idea," said a familiar manly voice. I looked up and saw Dhruv standing there, flipping the light brownish drumsticks between the fingers of his right hand. He smiled and reached out his left hand, "Your song." Placing my hand gently over his, I stood up. I put the guitar against the chair and asked, "What song?"

"You told me once that Naaz and you had a song. You didn't mention which one."

"Down we Fall by Drake Bell," I clicked my fingers together.

"There. Play that for her on your guitar."

"You're my drummer for tonight?"

"Indeed. All yours," he smiled a really goofy smile. The two of us looked at each other, silence except for the music in the background and the crowd roaring. He then snapped out of it and said as I looked into his eyes, completely mesmerized, "Heard it as soon as I said it." I shook my head and cleared my throat, I asked, "So can I count on you?"

"Count on me on this one. I won't disappoint. I promise you this," he smiled.

I sighed and looked at him with puppy eyes, "Don't break your promise. Please." He chuckled and gently bumped my right shoulder with his fist, and replied, "I promise." I managed a small smile and whispered, "Thanks, Dex. You're a great friend."

"Not a jackass anymore?" His eyes lit up.

"Always a jackass, idiot."

He wrapped his arms around me and pulled me in for a hug. I buried my head in his chest and felt his warm embrace – the first time I didn't snap at him for doing so. I shut my eyes close as he gently placed his chin on my head.

I heard him whisper, "Still your best friend."

I chuckled, my eyes still shut, "Not that I'm complaining."

He laughed lightly and hugged me tightly.

six.

The curtains swept across the floor as the Z siblings walked off stage. I took my position on stage, sitting on a wooden chair; I placed my guitar on my right thigh and held onto the fret-board. A mike was positioned in front of me. I turned around and saw Dhruv sitting on a chair, a metallic red-coloured drum-set surrounding him. He looked up at me and gave me a thumbs up, passing a smile. I smiled back and looked forward, the curtains blocking the view to the crowd. I closed my eyes and sighed slightly. I said to myself in my head, "For Naaz. Down We Fall." I then opened my eyes as I heard Ashwini announce, "And now, the final act of the evening, is my best friend and the-person-I-don't-hate-that-much, on guitar, and on drums, my another best friend. Please give it up for Nikita Achanta and Dhruv Jain." I saw Ashwini push the side of the curtain slightly and walk back. She walked into the right wing of the stage and held the files to her chest. I took a deep sigh and saw the curtains pull away, unravelling the crowd.

I leaned forward slightly and spoke into the mike, "Hi, everyone." I heard the whole crowd applaud as I completed speaking those two words. I chuckled and continued, "It is amazing to be the closing act of this wonderful evening, and, uh, to have been a part of the first ever 10th class farewell." Everyone clapped again. I smiled, "This first song is very dear to my heart. I always find songs that my best friends and I can relate to. And since I have five idiotic best friends, I have five songs. This one, though, is the most special of those five." I sighed. "Naaz,"

The crowd went silent.

"I've done many wrongs since the day we first met but if there's one thing I'm thankful for, is for that one lovely, blessed day when you walked up to me and said hi cheekily. And this song's for you."

I placed my fingers on the fret-board, pressing them against a particular major chord. I strummed the strings with my bare fingers and sang into the mike after five seconds, "You were so clever, you kept it together today. By the way, I'll no longer ignore you; I wanted to show you again, I'm your friend. Sometimes we just pretend."

I slid my hand down the fret-board, changing chords according to the lyrics of one of my all-time favourites. I closed my eyes in immense pleasure, loosing myself to the song, and I heard the drums kick in from Dhruv's side.

I continued to sing, "And all I can say is you saved me, changed all the things that have made me. Entertaining, thoughts are raining, down we fall."

I lowered my pitch. "It's all okay, when I say, you and I. Take your time; I can't wait to see you fly."

I increased my pitch again, still soft, "You don't have to wander, and I've finally discovered tonight, where we're all right."

I heard Dhruv and three backup singers sing along for the fading of words. I smiled, my eyes shut, and continued to sing, "This is just the beginning, and it's all that I'm trying to say, if I may, you're never in my way."

I heard the crowd, even the performers backstage and the people standing on the stage's unrevealing side, clap along to the lyrics of the song, "And all I can say is you saved me, changed all the things that have made me. Entertaining, thoughts are raining, down we fall."

I strummed slowly, reaching the end of the song, "It's all okay, when I say, you and I. Take your time; I can't wait to see you fly."

I opened my eyes slowly as I let go off the fret-board and dropped my hand to my knee. I saw and heard the whole crowd clapping and roaring with happiness. They were all standing up. I smiled and hoped, just hoped, on the inside, that Naaz was one of those people who were applauding me. I turned my head to the side and saw Ashwini clapping excitedly and frantically. I smiled at her and she smiled back, nodding her head in approval.

I flicked my hair to the side and spoke into the mike, "You all can sit down now. This isn't the end. Not yet."

seven.

The curtains were drawn but that wasn't the end. I stood up from my chair and a student came and picked up the chair, taking it to the side. I put my guitar against the chair and picked up a crimson-red Gibson electric guitar placed on a guitar stand. I put the guitar-strap around it and hung it around my neck, feeling light pressure on my left shoulder.

"Okay," I said as I pulled my shirt down. "Let's get this over with."

Dhruv was still sitting on the drums, flipping the drumsticks between his fingers. I plugged in a wire into the guitar which was connected to a black amplifier. I walked back on the stage and positioned the mike a little distant from my mouth, at my level.

I looked at Dhruv and asked, "You ready?"

He looked up at me, nodded and replied, "Ready."

I smiled and the curtains were pulled away and I smiled as the crowd roared once again. Everyone had taken their seats. I spoke into the mike, "Okay, this song is by a band that I completely obsessed over when I first heard their hit single on VH1, and I wouldn't shut up singing the song. And this is the song. And yes, I'm going to need a little help. I want all the girls and ladies in here to lightly clap on their thighs twice in one go, and when they stop, I want the guys and men to clap their hands together. Like in a rhythm. You guys get me?" The crowd screamed yes together. I smiled and continued, "Good."

I placed my fingers on the fret-board and heard Dhruv kick in the drums. I picked on the lower three strings alternatively and started off with the lyrics, "So this is what you meant when you said that you were spent? And now it's time to build from the bottom of the pit right to the top. Don't hold back, packing my bags and giving the academy a rain check."

I heard the sound of drumsticks clicking together, the sound of the crowd doing like I told them to, it felt great. I smiled and continued, shifting chords accordingly, I sang the words that touched me the most because of obvious reasons, "I don't ever want to let you down, I don't ever want to leave this town, 'cause after all, this city never sleeps at night."

I started off with the chorus of It's Time by Imagine Dragons, "It's time to begin, isn't it? I get a little bit bigger, but then, I'll admit, I'm just the same as I was. Now don't you understand, I'm never changing who I am?"

"So this is where you fell? And I am left to sell the path that heaven runs through miles of clouded hell, right to the top. Don't look back, turning to rags and give the commodities a rain check."

"I don't ever want to let you down, I don't ever want to leave this town, 'cause after all, this city never sleeps at night."

"It's time to begin, isn't it? I get a little bit bigger, but then, I'll admit, I'm just the same as I was. Now don't you understand, that I'm never changing who I am?

I closed my eyes towards the end of the song. "This road never looked so lonely... this house doesn't burn down slowly... to ashes... to ashes..."

I smiled as I opened my eyes and heard the crowd singing the chorus, "It's time to begin, isn't it? I get a little bit bigger, but then, I'll admit, I'm just the same as I was. Now don't you understand, that I'm never changing who I am?"

I sang and finished off the song with the last lyrics, "It's time to begin, isn't it? I get a little bit bigger, but then, I'll admit, I'm just the same as I was. Now don't you understand, that I'm never changing who I am?"

I looked around and let out a sigh of happiness as the crowd stood up and applauded. My heart went all dubstep and it started dancing crazily as I felt it beat faster.

That was my moment.

eight.

After putting both the guitars in their proper places, I walked down the stage and back into the crowd. Everyone I passed along told me that Dhruv and I performed great and that it was one of the best performances they'd seen in years. I was filled with contentment as I made my way past the crowd. I stopped as I saw Naaz standing in front of me. I wasn't sure as to how she would react, or how she reacted when I dedicated that song to her. I shoved my hands into my jeans' pockets and the two of us walked up to each other.

I said quietly, "Hi."

She looked down and said remorsefully, "I'm sorry. I overreacted." I chuckled and replied, "Now, this is one of those moments when I'm not going to say that you don't need to apologise."

"It's my fault?" She looked up at me.

"It's not anyone's fault. Didn't you hear the lyrics? You're never in my way. And neither would I ever dare to push you away. Maybe you haven't realised yet what kind of a person I really am."

"Then it is my fault."

"Darling, there's no shortage of fault to be found amid our stars."

She sighed and looked down again. I thought she was trying to comprehend what I just said meant.

"I'll see you later," I said as I walked past her. "I'm not in the best of forms either. So chill." She turned around and watched me walk away as I wore a blank expression.

Was I tired? Not likely. Too many memories were flooding back to me. Memories I'd wished I'd forget. But the universe doesn't work that way. Those memories tell you of your flaws and how people get hurt by your petty little words, no matter how much you say you didn't mean them.

As Dhruv would say, quoting John Green, "I believe the universe wants to be noticed."

nine.

We got over with the dinner, group photographs and personal photographs. Even I got a few clicked with my little group of friends and the teachers I liked. After that, everyone was bidding each other goodbye with promises that they'd see each other soon enough, which was true in most cases because all of them were staying in the same school for two more years. But untrue in my case. I saw the students hugging each other and making promises of never forgetting each other and staying friends forever and all that. And then there was me. I was sitting on a chair, looking at people, my left leg over my right knee. I saw Ashwini walk over and she plopped down on the chair left to me.

She looked at me and asked joyfully, "How come you're not making any promises tonight?" I chuckled and replied, looking down to the ground, "If you know me well, you already know the answer to that question."

She nodded her head and looked forward, resting her arm on my chair's back, "What is the deal with you, Nikita?"

"What is the deal with me?"

"Your faith in promises."

"I don't have any faith in promises."

"And why is that?" She looked at me, her eyes full of pity.

I looked back at her. "Promises break. They shatter. Like glass shattering inside of you. Now what if that glass gets through to your heart? What if that broken glass pierces your heart? What then?"

"...I don't have an answer to that."

I chuckled. "I've seen a lot of broken promises in my sixteen years on this planet. I don't want to see broken promises. Not anymore. I've felt my heart getting pierced by a knife. But not anymore."

"People made promises and they broke them. You're saying you haven't made any promises? You haven't broken any?"

"That's right. A lot of glass inside of me. Me? I never made promises. I haven't promised anything to anyone, which reduces the weight on my shoulders."

She sighed sadly and got up from her chair. She looked at me and said, "We should get going. It's getting late." I nodded my head and stood up from the chair. I picked up my guitar case which was leaning against the chair to my right. I already had my side-bag around my left shoulder. Ashwini and I walked up to Lakshita and Dhruv and the four of us were about to walk off the property. I stopped. Ashwini turned around and asked, "All okay?" I nodded my head and looked at all of them one by one. I chuckled a little and said, "Would it kill to ask for a group hug right now?" And as I finished the sentence, Lakshita rushed towards me and wrapped her arms around me, hugging me tightly. I laughed and Dhruv and Ashwini joined as well.

And I could not have wished for more. Perfect harmony.

ten.

"Hey, Dhruv?" I remember asking before the two of us parted ways that evening. "I never said thank you."

"And you'll never have to," I remember him smiling warmly.

part three.

one.

The next morning, I lay in my bed, sound asleep. I shifted under the blanket restlessly, like I was having a bad dream. I clenched my eyelids and my fists around the blankets. I then stopped moving and slowly opened my eyes. I rolled over and saw my mum arranging my clothes in my cupboard.

"Another one of those nightmares?" she asked with her back turned towards me.

I nodded my head and answered, "I have a bad feeling."

"What?" She turned around.

"Something tells me I shouldn't get out of bed this morning."

"Well, don't you feel like that every other day?"

"That is also true," I chuckled.

I sat up on the bed, the blanket covering down my waist. I stretched my arms and yawned as I shut my eyes tightly. I then rubbed my eyes and heard a knock on my room's door. Mum shut the cupboard's door and walked over to the door and opened it. I peeped over. Lakshita smiled and said, "Good morning, aunty." My mum smiled back and replied, "G'morning, Lakshita. Please, come in." Lakshita walked in and I waved at her. I reached for my glasses on my bedside and put them on.

"Coffee, Nikita?" mum asked. I nodded my head and replied, "One for Lex too, please." Mum smiled and walked out of my room, shutting the door behind her. I looked at Lakshita and asked, "What brings you here this early, lady?" Lakshita plopped down on the edge of the bed and replied in a whisper, "Rumours did." I raised my eyebrows and asked again, "What kind of rumours?"

"Students in my locality are saying that..." She stopped.

"Saying what?"

"Ashwini's your best friend, right?"

"Of course she is."

"And you know everything about her? She tells you everything?"

"I believe she does."

"Then this is going to sound really weird."

"I'll be the judge of that."

I folded my arms and looked at Lakshita as she spoke nervously, "Rumours say that Ashwini and Dhruv are going out." I gasped and my jaw dropped. That was something I did not expect to hear. Like, ever. I shook my head and asked, "What? W-where did you hear that?" She sighed and answered, "Everyone's saying it. I don't know if it's true or not, though." I broke into a fit of laughter and giggles as I dropped back on the bed, my hands on my stomach, trying to stop my laughter. Lakshita looked at me all weird and asked, "Err, dude?" I sat up and wiped the tears from my eyes. I replied as I stopped my laughter, "Ashwini and Dhruv? Your brother? Don't make me laugh. The two of us know very well of how much Ashwini despises Dex."

"Well, what if—"

"No what ifs, my friend. This case is closed. Dex and Ash aren't going out, and I'm sure of it."

"If you say so." She sighed.

"And besides, Dex's your brother. He'd definitely tell you if something was up. That I'm sure of. Plus, doesn't he have this puppy crush on me or something?"

"Yeah, I guess," She sighed once again as she nodded her head. I reached forward and placed my right hand gently on her left shoulder, and said comfortingly, "Don't worry. Ashwini would definitely tell us if all this was true." I passed her a reassuring smile. She nodded her head and managed a small smile.

"I sure hope she, or at least Dhruv, does," She said as she looked at me. "Or I'll kill both of them."

"You won't get the opportunity." I smirked. I just trusted the two of them, is all.

two.

Lakshita and I spoke to each other as we sipped on our coffees.

"I watched Inception last night," Lakshita said as she rested the cup of coffee on her right knee, while still sitting on my bed. I smiled and asked, "Lovely. Thoughts?" She trailed her left index finger along the cup's rim and replied, dreamily, "I ship Robert and Dom."

My jaw dropped. I was startled and confused. "You did not just say that you ship the very gorgeous Robert Fischer with Dom, right?"

"Yeah, I ship them." She nodded once.

"No, that's just...wrong." I replied, denial and opposition all over.

"You should ship them too. They're perfect together." She sighed dreamily.

"I just... no. You know very well that I can't ship Fischer with anyone because of how flawlessly gorgeous he is, let alone ship him with Cobb."

"But there's so much chemistry between them!"

"Keep my poor Fischer out of this, please. What has he ever done to deserve being shipped with Cobb? No, stop. Please. Just stop."

"They're a lovely pairing, no matter how much you hate them together."

"Dude – get out of here, of I'll murder you in your sleep," I said plainly as I looked at her.

She laughed manically and replied after a few seconds, "Okay, okay, I'm sorry." She flashed her puppy eyes and continued, "But that doesn't mean I don't ship them." I shrugged my shoulders and took a sip of my coffee. She then said, bringing her cup near her lips, "Speaking of weird ships," I looked at her and she questioned, "What's your opinion on ships from The Dark Knight Trilogy?" I shook my head lightly and answered, "I can't see myself shipping anyone with anyone, really. Apologies." I took another sip of my coffee and Lakshita said in a low pitch, "I ship Jonathan Crane and Rachel Dawes from Begins." I threw the coffee out of my mouth, in the form of a spray. Lakshita pulled back slightly. I then coughed for a few second as I wiped my lips. I asked, startled once again, "Dude, what even—"

"Have you seen how defensive they are when they come face-to-face after Zsaaz's hearing?" She gave me an obvious look. "It's like they're masking their feelings."

"I just—"

"And who knows what happened in that elevator scene in Begins, eh?"

"Yeah, thank you for that image, I needed that," I shrugged my shoulders in disgust.

"They're so gorgeous together."

"Uh, no. Just no. Like I said before, any-role-Cillian-plays is way too pretty to be shipped, with anyone. Cillian's way too beautiful to be shipped with his own wife, for heaven's sake! He's not human. He's an entirely different species. He's a god. A flawless, perfect god. He's legendary."

"Uh…" She gave me weird look.

I sighed and shook my head in disapproval. I replied, "It's like I've taught you nothing about pairings, ships and couples." She chuckled and said, "Seems like the great Nikita failed at something." I glared at her. She winked at me and took another sip of her coffee. I sighed and rolled my eyes in utter disgust.

I turned my head to the left and gazed at my Fangirl Wall. I let out a dreamy sigh. Lakshita looked at me and asked, "What are you thinking about?" I replied, my eyes still on the wall, "Liv Tyler." She narrowed her eyebrows and said, "Huh? I thought—" I interrupted, "And Cillian Murphy."

"Both at the same time?"

"Dude. Liv is so beautiful. She's, like, really very pretty, and Cillian's gorgeous. Why aren't the two of them together? They'd make great kids together. Their kids would be beautiful."

"Liv is the one from Armageddon, right?" She finished her coffee.

"Yeah, she's the one. The pretty, perfect one."

"She is beautiful. That's the only movie I've seen of her."

"I ship Livian so hard. Ciliv. No, Livian sounds better."

"Look I admit that your imagination is wonderful but for the sake of sanity—"

"But their kids will be beautiful. Liv and Cilly both have cheekbones, blue eyes and great hair. Those two need to get together, then I can marry one of their kids."

"Even if their kid is 16 years younger to you?" She chuckled.

"Age doesn't matter anymore." I closed my eyes and shook my head slowly.

"Right, age is just a number!" She exclaimed, a smile on her face.

"Yeah, but then again, jail is just a room."

"Sorry," she said with a sigh. I laughed lightly and replied, "Chill, lady. Speaking of perfection…" I put away my empty cup on my bedside and continued, "Think about it, if Jonathan Crane, in Batman Begins, spoke for all us fangirls." She blinked and looked at me, and asked, not getting a word of what I was saying, "Err…?"

"Would you like to see my mask? Covering my face probably wouldn't bother a guy like you, but these ladies, they can't stand it."

"I know what you're going to say next. In his—"

"In his sexy voice." I nodded my head and smirked mischievously. Lakshita chuckled and asked, "What are your thoughts about his movie, In Time?" I rolled my eyes and answered promptly, "In Time is such a crappy movie, man." She jumped up to her feet and shouted, pointing a finger towards me, "Lies! You've seen it a thous—" Before she could complete the sentence, I spoke in between, "But damn, does Cillian look good in tight leather pants!" She pouted and sat back on the bed slowly. I grinned. I bit into my right cheek and asked, "Can I admit something?"

"What, that you wish to stab me right now?" She perked up a bit.

"Nah. This is weird for me to admit, but I would love to be used by Dr. Jonathan Crane as a 'test subject'."

Lakshita looked into my eyes and whispered, "I just got that image and...wow." I nodded my head quickly, a smile tugged on my lips, and asked, "And the image is amazing, isn't it?" She nodded her head really quickly. I sighed happily and continued, "I think that casting Cillian Murphy as Dr. Jonathan Crane was the best decision Christopher Nolan ever made." Lakshita smiled happily and replied, "It sure was. Cillian Murphy is the perfect bad guy. He is perfection in every way possible." I scratched my left cheek and said, joy in my voice, "You just read my mind. I'll tell you this." I shifted lightly as I sat in my bed and continued, "So, my 8-year old nephew saw my iPhone screen of Cillian Murphy and he was all like, 'Oh, is that your boyfriend?' And I was like..." I nodded my head and quivered my lips as I finished the sentence, "'Mm-hmm.'" Lakshita started laughing and I laughed along with her.

"You know what?" she asked. I stopped laughing and pressed my lips together, and said, "What?"

"For some reason, the scenes from Batman Begins with Jonathan Crane in a straitjacket really turn me on."

I gasped and said, "Oh my god. Me too." She passed me a shark-like grin. I continued, my smile fading away, "But... there's this one thing that's horrible." I sighed.

"What's horrible?" She tilted her head to the left.

"I feel like the only person that finds Jonathan Crane sexy because of his complex mind."

"And for his looks?" She smiled softly and asked like a true fangirl. I looked up at her and chuckled, answering, "And for his drop-dead gorgeous looks, yes."

Lakshita kept her hand on my left shoulder and said, "Look; it's pretty clear that Cillian Murphy is the hottest villain that I have ever watched in a movie." I nodded my head in approval and said, grabbing her hand that was on my shoulder, "I know, right? He just pulls it off so well and you can't help but feel attracted to him. He's more captivating as an antagonist than he is as a protagonist." Lakshita nodded her head frantically and said in the same tone of excitement, "And this is why villains kick ass." I laughed lightly and pulled my hand back as she pulled hers.

"Dude. I find Cillian so sexy in a straitjacket." Dreamily, I gazed into the distance.

"That's because he is."

I shook my head, snapping out of it and looked at her and the two of us exchanged smiles. She then cupped both her cheeks with her hands and said, sliding them down slowly, "And cheekbones. Oh my god." I flailed and replied, "Cheekbones are bloody attractive. Cheekbones plus eyes plus messy hair equals to perfection, which equals to Cillian Murphy, Ben Whishaw, Tom Hiddleston, Benedict Cumberbatch, Johnny Depp, James McAvoy, Tom Felton and Tom Cruise." Lakshita pulled her hands off her cheeks and asked, "And Dhruv Jain?" I snapped out of my daze and gave her a stern look as I lightly punched her right shoulder. Lakshita chuckled and then looked at the little golden watch around her left wrist. She said as she looked at it, "I should really get going now." She stood up from my bed and walked over, placing the empty coffee cup on my bedside table. I got up from my bed, slipping my feet into my slippers.

The two of us walked down the stairs and then out of my house. She sat on her activa and smiled at me as she pushed in the key into the ignition hole. I folded my arms and said happily, "I had fun." She looked up at me. I continued, "You should come over more often, so that we can fangirl over the perfection of our favourite celebrities."

"Will do, mate." She nodded her head and chuckled.

"I'm just glad there's someone in this town who shares my obsessions."

"You've no idea how blessed I feel to have you as my best friend."

"The feeling's the same over here," I smiled at her as she turned her activa around. She turned her head around and said, "I'll text you later."

I nodded my head and waved at her as she drove off after passing me a wide smile.

three.

It was three in the afternoon and I sat on my beanbag, reading 'John Dies at the End' by David Wong. My bare feet were placed on the bed and Paramore's album Riot! was playing on my iPod placed on the JBL dock. I tapped my feet lightly together as I read the book and moved my head to the songs' beats. I then heard a knock on the door. I looked at the door and rolled my eyes. I got up as I put the 470 pages book down on the bed. I picked up the dock's remote from the beanbag and paused the music. I walked up to the door and opened it.

There stood Ashwini, looking a little cross. I flashed my usual smile and said, "Oh hey." She looked up at me and said, almost a whisper, "You're such a liar." My smile faded away. I raised up a brow and asked, "I'm sorry, what was that again?"

"Stop with the innocence, will you?" She frowned.

"You're not getting to the point."

"You spread the rumours."

"Pardon me, but what?"

She rolled her eyes and answered, "You heard me! You spread those rumours that Dhruv and I are dating. How low can you stoop, Nikita?" I chuckled, thinking she was joking, and questioned again, "Why would I even do that?" She shrugged her shoulders and answered, yet again, "How in hell do I know what goes on in your messed-up head?" I said calmly, trying not to lose my temper, "I did not spread those rumours. I got to know about them this mor—" Before I could continue my sentence, Ashwini interrupted by saying, "You don't mean half the things you say." I lost it and replied, "So I didn't spread those rumours! Who even told you I did?"

"Some guys told me." She bit her lower lip.

"Really, now? You're willing to believe Tom, Dick and Harry, and not your bloody best friend?!"

She moved up closer to me and said, "Because with your sickass attitude, it doesn't work in the real world, Nikita. Just as self-centred, arrogant, ignorant and heartless, just like your brother and—" I lost all control and yelled, "Don't say a word against my brother! You barely know him!" I sighed and I looked away. I then continued, looking straight into her eyes, "I hate you. So much." She was about to say something but I stopped her and said, dead serious, "And I do mean that."

"Nikita, it doesn't have to—"

"Now get your bloody feet off my father's property before I land a punch in your face."

She looked at me all confused. I shut the door in her face and tugged at the tips of my hair in anger. I clenched my eyes and leaned against the cream wall. I held my head in my hands and slid down the wall. I sat on the marble floor, my head in my hands, my eyes shut tight.

"That did not happen," I said to myself, trying to convince myself that it was all a bad dream, but it wasn't. I pulled my hands down and looked up at the ceiling.

As Dhruv would say, quoting John Green, "The marks humans leave are too often scars."

four.

It was five in the evening.

"She was just not in a good mood, Nikita," said Naaz as the two of us sat in an open cafeteria down the block. I took a sip of my Irish Coffee and replied coldly, "Whatever it was. She said stuff, I said stuff. It's all over now." I looked away as I cupped the cup with my hands. Naaz sighed and said, taking a bite of her cheese burger, "Really? You flush three years of friendship down the drain just because she said something while she was angry?"

"She accused me. And if you know me well, I was done dealing with false accusations three months ago." I gave her a stern look.

"It's not about being accused. She's your best friend."

"Was my best friend. Was my friend."

"You're going to break it off like that?"

I looked into her eyes as she looked back into mine.

"Nikita, dude!" I turned around in my chair as I heard a familiar feminine voice. It was Lakshita. She rushed up to me with Dhruv behind her. I rolled my eyes and asked, "What are you two doing here?" Lakshita pulled a chair from the table next to ours and sat down to my left. She replied, "Naaz called." I looked over at Naaz as Lakshita completed the sentence. Naaz looked down, covering her face with her hands, trying to avoid eye contact with me. I shook my head and leaned back into my chair. Dhruv leaned his right hand against the back of Lakshita's chair and asked, "What's up between you and Ashwini?" I glared at him and replied, "There is nothing up. Just stay out of it." He shrugged his shoulders and shoved his right hand into his brown three-fourths' pocket. Naaz looked up slightly and said nervously, her eyes rising, "Uh-oh." I turned around in my chair once again and saw Ashwini walk in, her eyes on her phone. I got up from my chair and gave her a stern look. Lakshita and Naaz stood up as well, facing Ashwini. Ashwini looked up and asked, walking up to us, "What are you doing here?"

"Well, the last time I checked, you did not own this cafeteria."

"Why is it that wherever I go, you go?"

"I did not ask you to come here. Actually, I'd rather leave than be in the same room as you."

She folded her arms and frowned, her eyes cross. I continued, with a little unpleasant smirk covering my lips, "Honestly, I don't want to be around you. I don't want you in my vicinity." She looked at me with a weird look, tilting her head to the left. I said, ". I don't even want you in my city. If I could move to Jupiter, I would, but I wouldn't be able to breathe." She raised her hands up into the air and replied, angrily, "You kno—I'll just leave."

"I'll show you out myself."

"Oh, wouldn't that be just perfect."

She turned around and walked up to the door. I walked behind her and watched her as she walked out on to the street. I walked out as well and leaned against the glass door. I watched Lakshita, Dhruv and Naaz walk out of the door as well. Ashwini made her way half across the road and then stood in the centre, turned around me and yelled, "I'll just get out of your environment." As she went on, I heard a buzzing noise coming from the right. I then looked up at Ashwini and said to myself, "A speeding car." I increased my pitch, "Ashwini, get out of the way." She gasped and replied, "Oh, so now I'm in your way? Lovely!" I looked to my right and saw a speeding black Honda City approach.

"Ashwini, watch out!" I yelled as I ran towards her, jumped lightly into the air and grabbed her by her shoulders, pushing her out of the car's way as I shut my eyes tightly, trying not to get hit by accident. The car screeched, veered as it nearly missed us. I figured the driver had pushed on the brakes and yanked the wheel as the tires screeched. The car brushed past us as I pushed Ashwini out of the way and we tumbled down some concrete steps. She hit her head against the concrete pavement as the two of us landed on the ground, lying there. I tilted my head back against the floor, clenching my eyelids tightly, I placed my right hand on my neck.

"That's gotta hurt," I said to myself. "But it'll pass." I sat up and pulled my hand back, then placed it on my left wrist, groaning slightly. I sighed deeply and opened my eyes, feeling numbness in my wrist. I looked over and saw Ashwini as she sat up, holding her right hand to her head. She moaned. I saw blood dripping from the right side of her forehead. I held onto my wrist and asked, "You alright?" She shook her head, her eyes shut tight, she was barely able to open her mouth, but still she replied, "No, not really." I stood up, trying not to stumble, and said, breathing heavily, "We have to get you to the hospital." She looked up at me and asked, her voice almost a slur, "Since when did you start to care again?"

"I do not. But I have a possibly broken wrist here and I really want to go see a doctor."

"As expected: You're thinking of no one but yourself."

We couldn't stop arguing even when Ashwini sat there, injured. I frowned and replied, "First off, be thankful that I saved your life. I risked mine for you." She shrugged her shoulders and sat there, burying her head in her hands. I sighed and cooled down slightly. I then said, "Get up, now, come on." I looked around and then back at her as she said, shaking her head lightly, "I-I can't."

"I'm not taking melodrama anymore. Get up on your feet now."

"I can't. My head feels like it's about to bu— "

Before she could complete the sentence, I saw her eyes closing gently as she fell to the ground, unconscious. I widened my eyes and kneeled down next to her, placing my right hand on her neck, I whispered, "Hold on, I'm getting you out of here."

five.

I sat on a bench in the hospital corridor. I rubbed my hands together as thoughts rushed through my head and people walked by. The corridor was filled with voices but I couldn't hear any. They were all a blur. I looked over at the crepe-bandage that covered my sprained left wrist. I sighed and then looked around before leaning back into the bench. Dhruv came and sat next to me and let out a deep sigh. I looked over at him as he wore an expression of agitation. He folded his left leg over his right knee and looked back at me.

"You think she'll be alright?" I asked him curiously. He passed me a comforting smile and answered, "Of course, she'll be alright. She'll pull through. She always does." I nodded my head and looked over at the red light on the Operation Theatre sign. I sighed. Dhruv got up from the bench and said, looking at his watch, "We should go now." Lakshita walked up to him after she finished speaking with a nurse. I stood up from the bench and nodded my head. Lakshita leaned forward and hugged me lightly, trying not to hurt my broken wrist. I hugged her back, patting her back with my right hand. She pulled away and whispered, "Call me if you need anything." I nodded my head, my face deprived of expressions. I then looked over at Dhruv as Lakshita walked away, leaving the two of us to talk.

Dhruv scratched his right cheek and sighed. Looking into my eyes, he said softly, "I'm just glad I didn't lose you."

I chuckled and replied, "You're never going to lose me. I'm not dying." I passed him a reassuring smile.

He nodded his head with a quiet smile covering his lips. He said, "I don't want to lose you."

I was lost for words as I gazed into his eyes, I then said, breaking the silence, "I'll text you later." He nodded his head and leaned forward, placing a small kiss on my left cheek. I closed my eyes as he whispered, "You take care." I turned around as I watched him walk out of the hospital.

I sat on the hospital bench, my feet folded onto the bench. I sighed lightly as I gazed up blankly at the white ceiling. I then heard footsteps and looked to my left as I saw Naaz, with a paper bag, walk up to me. I stood up from the bench and asked out of curiosity, "What are you doing here? I sent you home." She nodded once and replied, "I didn't go home. I figured you'd stay back at the hospital since Ash's family isn't in town, so I got you some pasta packed from the cafeteria." She smiled at me and I said a little hesitantly, "Yeah, thanks." I half-smiled as I took the paper bag from her, putting it on the bench gently. I looked back at her and she said, "I'm staying, in case you're wondering." She sat down on the bench. I looked at her, dazed, and replied, "Y-you can't. You should go home. You need rest." She looked up at me and shook her head stubbornly. I chuckled and flopped down on the bench next to her. I sighed and buried my face in my hands. I then heard Naaz say, "Life's so unpredictable." I looked up at her and she continued, "Better seize the moment." I sighed and asked, "What are you trying to tell me?"

"Like you're totally oblivious to it; Dhruv," she said, rolling her eyes as she saw my eyes go inanimate.

"What about him?" I gulped.

"Despite the little act you put up, trying to fool everyone that you have no feelings for him whatsoever, you might fool everyone but you can't fool yourself," her voice sounded heavy. She breathed heavily. "Ashwini could have died. It could have been you in her place. So please, just don't—"

I stopped her from finishing her sentence and I said, "I get what you're saying."

Naaz chuckled and said, clearing her throat, "As Dhruv would say, quoting John Green, 'In the end, we're only humans drunk on the idea that love, only love, can heal our brokenness.'"

She smiled and that one sentence made me rethink the entire five-year friendship I'd shared with Dhruv.

six.

I yawned as I shifted in the bench's chair in which I slept. I opened my eyes slightly and looked over to my side to find Naaz reading 'The Fault in Our Stars' by John Green. I stretched my arms and looked around with an eye closed. The lights were all dimmed in the corridor and there was no one around, just a nurse sitting at the reception. I looked back at Naaz and asked, "She out of the OT yet?" She looked at me and nodded her head, replying, "She's been out for over an hour. I didn't want to wake you up." I let out a long yawn and then questioned, "Where is she?" Naaz pointed to a room about ten feet away from me. I stood up and stretched my body as she got back to reading her book again.

I walked to the room and opened the door, peeking in through it. I walked inside and gently closed the door behind me. I walked up to the bed in which Ashwini lay, her breathing steady, a white bandage wrapped around her forehead. I kneeled down near the bed and looked at her face as she lay there with her eyes shut.

I sighed slightly and said, assuming she was able to listen, "You know, this could have been much serious." I swallowed and continued, "I saved your life."

I chuckled. "I feel so glad I did, even if I broke my wrist in doing that." I looked up at her and took a hold of her right hand, holding it in between both my hands. "And you said I cared about no one else but me. I guess it's true. I don't. I'm arrogant, self-centred, ignorant. I'm so many things that I surprise myself every day. So here's the deal – no more melodrama, you have to get up, okay? For me. Do that for me." I felt a weird lump at the back of my throat, the one a person gets before crying. But I was not going to cry. I bit my lower lip. "I know we said things to each other. Things we didn't mean. But best friends have fights, don't they? And they always get through." I looked away and stood up as I heard no reply. I let go off her hand and watched it fall down on the bed.

I turned around to leave but stopped as I heard a weak voice from behind, "So you don't really hate me?" I turned around on my heels and smiled slightly as I watched Ashwini looking at me with sleepy and tired eyes. I chuckled and replied, "I do, but not as much. Not the whole of you."

"You saved my life." She smiled slightly.

"I had to. You'd do the same, right?"

"I'd never have the guts to do that. I'd cry over a broken wrist, that I can guarantee."

"So typical of you." I chuckled.

She moved in her bed and sighed.

"Get some rest," I said as I looked at her pitifully. "You need it." She looked back at me and asked, "Don't you need it?" I shook my head and replied, "I'm right outside if you need me. Good night." She passed me a soft smile and said, "Good night, Nikita." I smiled as I backed out of the room, shutting the door behind me.

I sighed happily at the thought that she was recovering, and that she'd get better and back to her normal annoying self in a few days' time.

seven.

a week later...

It was the 1st of April and I sat on the swing in the park, making bubbles by blowing through a small hole dipped in a soap solution, holding the little plastic hoop with my broken left wrist. Bubbles flew across and over my head and I smiled at the sight of them. I sat there, gazing at the clear blue sky, watching clouds hover across. I sighed slightly and then heard a voice from behind, "Hey you." I blinked and turned my head around, just to find Lakshita standing behind me. I smiled and replied, "Hi." She walked over and sat on the swing next to me.

"I had a feeling I'd find you here," she said as she gripped the metal chains that hung the swing. She kicked her feet lightly and started to swing, bobbing back and forth. I looked at her and said, "I'll take it you know me well."

"Considering it's Monday, and we have our holidays, I'd figured you'd have nothing better to do." She laughed lightly.

"Wow, I don't even know how that takes up on my reputation." I shook my head.

"Chill. As for me, I have a craving right now."

"Do tell, Lex."

"I want pizza. Like, right now."

"I want Cillian Murphy but we don't always get what we want."

She laughed as she pushed her head back, gazing up at the sky as she swung, and replied, "Always so mature, aren't you?" I smiled charmingly and said cockily, "Always so charming, mademoiselle." She nodded her head as she tilted her head towards me. I looked around and saw Dhruv walking over. My smile faded away and I quickly pulled out my earphones from my jeans' pocket, along with my iPhone. I quickly put the earphones in my ears and put on 'Lovesick Melody' by Paramore, by double tapping the home button on my iPhone and then clicking play. I tapped my feet lightly on the ground, humming along with the song, pretending I never saw Dhruv approaching. I was in no mood for confrontation – especially after that conversation I'd had with Naaz. Lakshita laughed again, giving me a silly look. I kept the volume low enough to listen to their voices. Dhruv walked over and greeted with a smile, "Hey, you two." I waved my hand at him lightly as he gave me a weird look, quivering his lower lip and raising his left eyebrow.

"Nikita?" he said. "Hey, Nikita?" He put his hand on my shoulder and shook me gently. I looked up at him and rolled my eyes. I pulled out both my earphones and paused the music. "Let's set some ground rules here," I said, my voice commanding. "Both earphones in: don't talk to me."

"Okay." He nodded.

"One earphone in: don't talk to me."

"Uh-huh."

"No earphones in: don't talk to me."

Dhruv now looked absolutely puzzled. Lakshita's swing came to a standstill and she laughed out loud. I looked at her and laughed as well.

"Dude, what?" I questioned, trying to stop myself from laughing. She shook her head lightly, still laughing, and replied, "You give my poor brother a hard time." I nodded my head as I folded my arms. Dhruv rolled his eyes and said, "Real mature, Nikita." I looked at him and winked. He shook his head and said excitedly, "I have a fun fact for you guys." Lakshita and I looked at him and I replied with a smirk, "Shoot." He coughed slightly and said in the same tone of excitement as before, "Harry Styles suffers wardrobe malfunction just before any 1D concert." Lakshita looked at him dazzled. I shrugged my shoulders and said jokingly, "Humph, looks like he needs a 'Swift' tailor." Lakshita and Dhruv, both, looked at me weirdly as I stifled a laugh. I looked at both of them one by one, saying, "Swift tailor? Get it? Swift? Tailor? Oh, forget it." I pouted. Lakshita and Dhruv exchanged looks and then burst out laughing. I chuckled and said, trying not to laugh, "You guys are so mature." I stopped smiling and then my look turned into one of seriousness. I sighed deeply, reeking of exasperation. Dhruv looked at me and asked, puzzled, "All okay there, Nikita?"

"Something's missing." I shook my head.

"You, Lakshita and me, having a good time. What's missing?"

"I—nothing."

"We're the perfect trio, y'know."

I looked at him and managed a small smile, and replied, "I know." I stood up from the swing and walked away from the swingset slowly, shoving my hands into my jeans' pockets and looking down. Lakshita ran up from behind and asked, walking on my right, "Ashwini is missing, that's what, right?" I looked at her and shook my head, "Uh... not really, but— " Dhruv came up on my left and looked at me, asking, "Naaz is missing, that's what?" I looked at him and replied, "No, I was saying—" Lakshita snapped her right hand's fingers together and said like an idea struck her, "Both of them are missing! That's what Nikita's missing!" I stopped and clenched my fists. Closing my eyes tightly, I yelled, "No! Shut up, both of you!" The two of them gave me a blank look and I opened my eyes. I sighed and said, "The only thing that's missing is..." I looked at the curiosity in their eyes. I savoured the moment and continued slowly, "The thing... that's missing... is... coffee!" Lakshita dropped her shoulders almost immediately and asked, "That's it?" Dhruv chuckled and folded his arms, rolling his eyes playfully. I laughed lightly and said, "Got both of you, didn't it." They nodded their heads, Lakshita in amusement and Dhruv as he chuckled.

eight.

After half an hour, Lakshita sat on a metal bench in the park. I lay my head gently on her lap, gazing up at the sky. Dhruv sat on the grass, plucking the grass around him, bit by bit.

"You know what?" Lakshita said as she gently stroked my hair. I looked up at her and she continued, "I kind of want to speak my mind out right now."

I closed my eyes and snuggled into her lap. Nodding my head, I said, "Go ahead." She sighed deeply and said, tugging lightly at the roots of my hair, "I wonder what it feels like to be one of those pretty girls that all of the guys want." I opened my eyes almost instantly and looked at her, giving her an expression of dude-what-the-hell. Dhruv turned his head towards her but said nothing. I chuckled and replied, "I wonder what it feels like to be a unicorn." Dhruv let out a laugh, scratching his right cheek. Lakshita frowned and stuck her tongue out at me playfully. I sighed happily and shut my eyes again. Dhruv snapped his left hand's fingers together and asked, "If there was a zombie apocalypse right now, how'd you guys feel?" Lakshita pulled her hands away from my hair and cupped both her cheeks, pulled up a face of exasperation, and answered Dhruv's question as she flinched, "There's a zombie attack? I hate zombies!"

"If they want brains, you're safe, Lex." I chuckled.

"Offensive." She frowned.

"You can't even defend yourself. Me? I've trained my entire life for a zombie apocalypse."

"And how is that?"

"You are looking at a professional Xboxer. I'm a professional girl-gamer. I've spent half of my life killing people virtually, and murdering most muggles mentally. A zombie apocalypse will be a piece of cake for me."

She nodded her head, brushing my hair off my forehead, and said, "Oooooooof course." Dhruv chuckled and stood up, dusting away the grass from his jeans. He then said, pulling his phone out from his right pocket, "I'll be right back." He smiled and walked off. I opened my eyes and looked up as Lakshita as she looked into the distance. I asked, "Lex?"

"Yeah, Nixter?" She looked back at me.

"Remember that guy you told me of? Roman? The student from the exchange programme last year? The guy from Britain? You said you had a crush on him."

"I remember. What of him?" She chuckled.

"Have you gotten over him yet?"

"Not yet, but I will, eventually. Nikita?"

"Hmm?"

"Do you have any idea how much it hurts to love someone who you know will never love you back?"

I squirmed. "Dude. I am a fangirl. My entire life revolves around loving people who will never love me back. Some of them aren't even real people! They're fictional characters. Do you have any idea how sexually frustrating that is?!"

She looked at me, dazzled with widened eyes. I chuckled and shut my eyes, the ghost of a smile tugged at my lips. She laughed lightly and replied, "I'm a fangirl too. I feel you." I nodded my head, folding my right leg over my left knee as I lay on the bench.

"But then again," I heard Lakshita say. "All boys are the same, Nikita."

"Yes, because Johnny Depp, Obama and Adolf Hitler share extreme similarities." I rolled my eyes.

She grinned and then chuckled, humming slightly as she continued to stroke my hair gently. I opened my eyes gently and said, sighing slightly, "But the answer to your question..." She fixed her gaze at me. I continued, "...about loving someone who'll never love you back? I don't know how that feels like, but I guess it's like drowning, except you can see everyone around breathing."

"That's one way to put it." She exhaled a little loudly and patted my forehead.

I sighed and pulled my iPhone out of my jeans' right hip-pocket. "I'll tell Naaz to join us, if she can," I said as I unlocked my iPhone and typed a message to Naaz. I lay my head back again after I heard the 'delivered' beep. My iPhone vibrated and I looked at it. Lakshita asked, "What does she say?" I sighed deeply and replied, "She texted me saying 'K'."

"You're kidding me." Her look turned pale.

"I'm not. Such a moron."

"What are you going to reply?"

"Hmm." I put my fingers on the mini-keyboard. "K? K what? The letter before L, the letter after J? Did you know that in JK, K stands for 'kidding'? So your reply is 'kidding'? Or K as in Potassium? Do you need some Special K in your breakfast? K, as in K/O you? Can I knock you out and feed you to hungry sharks? Sharks has K in it."

Lakshita laughed out loudly as she heard me say what I was going to send Naaz. I pressed the send button and shoved my iPhone back into my pocket. I chuckled as I looked at Lakshita, who now covered her mouth with her hands, trying to control herself from laughing further.

"Oh, shut up," I said, slapping her face lightly.

nine.

the next day...

I sat on the black couch in our lobby. It was around eleven in the morning. I stared at my laptop's screen, as it lay on the table in front of me, a word document opened up but with no words in it. My iPhone was connected to the laptop through the white Apple cable. I sighed as I put my fingers on the keyboard, not getting any ideas on what to write, though. I sighed again, deeper this time. I started to type, turning on the bold and italic format settings. I was about to hit my fingers on the L key but then stopped as my iPhone vibrated. Without looking at the caller ID, I picked up the iPhone and put it to my ear.

"Achanta here," I said.

"Been too long, Nikita," said a familiar voice. It was Ashwini's.

I smiled slightly. "It has been. How are you feeling?"

"Never better. Head still hurts but I'll be fine."

"That's great."

"I'll have to talk to you later now. Bye!"

"Hey, wait—" Before I could say anything, she hung up. I sighed and looked at the iPhone's screen with narrowed eyes. I put it back on the table and leaned back into the couch.

I knew something was wrong. But I said nothing.

I picked up my laptop after shutting its lid down and got up and walked up to my room. I shut the door behind me and put my laptop on my beanbag. I sighed deeply and crashed on my bed. I rolled over and stared at the ceiling. I waited for my iPhone to vibrate and tell me that there was a text from Ashwini but it didn't go that way.

I waited desperately.

For minutes.

For hours.

I felt my iPhone vibrate for a second. I got up and sat up on my bed as I pulled my iPhone out from my pocket. It was a text from Ashwini. I smiled as I slid to unlock and. My smile faded away.

Will have to talk later. Apologies. – AK
You just got out of hospital. Can't I even ask how you've been? – NA
I said later, no. – AK
What's happened? – NA
What makes you think something's happened? – AK
You're behaving differently. Not like you were before. – NA
Before the accident? Yeah, right. – AK
Ashwini. Dude. What's happened? – NA
Nothing has. Just leave me alone, will you? – AK

My jaw dropped at those words. I was like, "What in the name of Sweet Mary was that?" I frowned and decided to put down my iPhone and not text her. I kicked back in bed, pushing my head back into the pillow. I gazed up at the ceiling, crossing my arms in anger. I closed my eyes, trying not to think of Ashwini. I then looked to my right, at my electric guitar which was leaning against the bedside table. I took hold of the fret board with my right hand and picked it up, arm's muscles clenched because it was heavy. I put it next to me on the bed and closed my eyes again, hugging the guitar.

I knew something was up. But what exactly?

ten.

I opened my eyes as I heard a knock at my door. I looked up and yawned.

"Come in," I said in a high pitch. I saw mum peek through the slightly-opened-door. She said with a smile, "Someone's here to see you." I sighed deeply and shook my head lightly, and said, "No offence, mum, but I really am not in the mood to see anyone right now, unless it's Liv Tyler, Johnny Depp or Cillian Murphy. I'm not interested." I buried my face in my hands and rubbed my palms against my face.

"What's it with you and socialising with people?" She rolled her eyes.

"It's not that I have a problem with socialising. People, in general, annoy me."

"Get on your nerves and tear you apart?"

I pulled my hands away from my face and looked at her, clapping my hands, "Yes, and with that, I'd like to end this conversation by saying that I do not wish to see anyone, thank you." I picked up my guitar and lay it in my lap as I sat cross-legged on the bed. I scooted back, pressing my back against the headboard. I took hold of the fret board with my left hand and strummed random tunes.

"Really?" I heard a familiar voice question. I looked up and saw Mini ma'am smiling at me.

I managed a small smile and said, "Hi. Come in." She walked in and shut the door behind her.

"You really didn't want to see me?" She asked again.

I shook my head quickly, smirking slightly. "Forget I said anything." I picked on the guitar strings as I continued, pointing to the beanbag, "Please, sit." She smiled slightly and walked up to the bed and sat down on the brown beanbag next to it. I stopped strumming and looked up at her and asked, "What are you doing here? No offence."

She chuckled. "I was just passing by. Thought I'd check up on you."

I smiled sheepishly. "Well, that's very nice of you. Thanks."

"And you don't seem yourself, yes?" She leaned back into the beanbag and watched me curiously.

I sighed deeply and looked at my guitar, running my left hand's fingers up and down the fret board. I then looked up at her and nodded, chewing on my lower lip as I answered, "I've been off the edge several times before, don't worry about me." She tapped her right foot gently on the carpet laid on the floor and she wore the ghost of a quiet smile. I looked at her again and she said, "Yeah, I get it. I heard Ashwini met with an accident. I'm sorry."

"She's well now. I saved her life." I smiled a little, then continued as my smile faded away, "But why are you sorry?" I let my gaze downcast and folded my right knee, hugging it with my hands, my chin pressing against the guitar's crimson body, my left leg still crossed.

"And you're not completely satisfied or happy by that."

My eyes widened slightly and I asked, "I'm sorry?"

"You heard me." She grinned cockily.

I let out a deep sigh and averted my gaze. I replied, "Okay. I admit I'm not as happy as I thought I would be." She leaned forward and folded her arms across her chest, listening intently. I looked at her and continued, "Ashwini and I haven't been on the best of terms lately."

"Let me guess," she interrupted. "You care for her, a little more than you should, and she doesn't. Well, she does, but not that much."

I nodded once. "I'm always playing up to her needs, even when I just want to be myself. And I have this problem: if the person does not reciprocate the love, I stop caring." I let out a chuckle. "Tell me how stupid that sounds, please."

"It doesn't," she said reassuringly.

I nodded my head once and continued, "Yeah. Sometimes, I just feel that she could do better without someone like me. And these thoughts don't come often to me, but they are today. And I'm not drunk or anything when I say this; I'm just high on the idea that I have eyes."

She looked at me and asked, "You're not depressed, are you?"

I bit my lower lip. "I'm just gonna come out with it today. I'm not sure if I'm depressed. I mean, I'm not sad.

But I'm not exactly very happy either. I mean, I haven't been since—" I stopped.

"Since?" She looked into my eyes as I looked at her.

I took a deep breath. "Last summer. I don't know what happened to me or what, up until then, I was more like a pseudo figure. Faking smiles. Faking laughter. Harbouring the unspoken pain inside," I swallowed hard before continuing, "Playing up to everyone's needs and expectations. I was fed up of constantly being unhappy. I mean, I know life's not supposed to be simple, but all I ever seemed to be doing was making everyone else happy, and I was just left feeling like nothing. And then I suddenly dropped it. I don't know what changed me, it just happened. It was like I woke up one morning and decided to be more like myself. I pushed loads of people away. I stopped caring about almost everything. Specific things started to make me smile, and not random things." I paused for a moment. "I changed. For the better."

She sighed deeply and said, "Everyone has to let go of things when the right time comes." I nodded my head real quick and replied, "It's like I'm six feet from the edge and I'm falling down." I bit into my right cheek as I continued, looking at her, "Look, I can laugh and joke and smile and pretend as if nothing's wrong and that I lead a perfectly happy teenage life during the day, but sometimes, when I'm alone at night, I forget how to feel. And that's just – it's all wrong." She looked back at me and smiled slightly, whispering, "It's not wrong. You're just discovering your inner self or something. You're human. It's all normal." I nodded my head slowly, looking away and thinking to myself. She then continued, leaning back into the beanbag, "So tell me more about what's going on between you and Ashwini." I looked at her and narrowed my eyes slightly. I took a deep breath once again and said meekly, "I'm starting to think she doesn't care about me anymore."

She widened her eyes slightly and stifled a laugh. "Ashwini? And not care about you? Really funny."

"I'm serious." I looked at her sternly.

"You still care about her, though, don't you?"

"I wish to stop myself from doing so, but it just doesn't work. Why should I care about someone who doesn't give a fuck about me?" I scratched my right cheek and averted my gaze.

"What makes you think she doesn't care about you anymore?"

I clenched my jaw and gritted my teeth, putting forward an answer to her question, "It's like I'm not talking to Ashwini. It's like I'm talking to a masked figure, that's hiding the real Ashwini behind it. She's not herself with me." She questioned once again, "Did you ask her if something's wrong?"

I shook my head. "I did. She said it's nothing."

"Do you believe—"

I interrupted. "I don't believe her."

"Did you talk to—"

I shook my head again, chuckling softly, "Neither do I wish to speak to her about this."

I then looked at her as she questioned, "How will you solve the problem if you don't speak to her about this?" She looked at me and waited patiently for an answer.

I looked away towards my Fangirl Wall and sighed, answering, "I'm gone in a month or two. What does it matter?" A parade of questions came rushing in from her, "Are you at peace with yourself?"

"I'm at peace with myself." I nodded.

"Do you feel happy and calm inside?"

I snickered. "I feel calm inside, don't know about happy. I'm not happy most of the times, so it doesn't matter."

"Do you want to care?" She asked.

"N—" I looked at her almost instantly before completing my answer. One word that almost escaped my lips unintentionally. I clenched my jaw tightly and buried my face in my hands.

"No?" I heard her ask.

"I don't know." I looked up at her, dropping my hands down. "Please don't ask me anymore questions." She shrugged her shoulders slightly, raising up both her eyebrows, and then dropping them immediately, saying, "Okay." I unclenched my jaw and looked at her, speaking out of the blue, coming clear with everything, "She thinks some of my habits undermine my 'dignity' and 'reputation', or whatever." Mini ma'am looked at me as I continued, "Like, if I don't give academics importance even for just a second, she gets really mad at me. I mean, why should I even think of studying when I'm reading a novel I love or playing my guitar? She sucks away half of the fun when I'm with her. And that makes me really angry and frustrated, like I don't want anything to do with her."

"She doesn't let you have fun when you want to?" She asked.

I nodded my head and answered, "Most of the time, and that makes me question my motives and actions." Mini ma'am took a deep breath and questioned, "Nikita, do you know why I teach?" I narrowed my eyes as I looked at her through my full-rimmed glasses. I shrugged my shoulders. She pulled up a smile and continued, "For the fun of it. Why would anyone do something for anything else?"

I pouted slightly and pushed my tongue into my left cheek "Okay, no offence, but how is teaching fun?" I questioned. "You're surrounded by kids who keep whining all the time about how they don't have an iPad, and who don't even care about you. At least, no one in my generation cares about anyone." I looked down as I clenched my feet's toes.

Mini ma'am shook her head in disapproval. She leaned forward and took a hold of my right hand with her left. I looked at her, my lips parting slightly. She looked back at me and said, "It's still fun, even if you are surrounded by people who don't care about you or those to whom you may seem boring. Even if Ashwini, or anyone else, criticises you, why should that stop you from doing something you love?" I nodded my head and tilted my head to the right, thinking. I then said out loud, "I guess that makes sense." She smiled and patted the back of my hand, pulling her hand back; she leaned back into the beanbag. I rubbed my right hand with my left and let out a sigh of happiness. I felt kind of happy inside, getting all that stuff off my chest.

"Can I ask something?" Mini ma'am asked.

"Anything, please."

She hesitated a little as I looked at her. She sighed and then finally asked with a sweet smile on her face, "How long before you turn this into a book?"

I widened my eyes slightly in surprise. I nodded once and replied, a smile covering my lips, "Sooner than you think, mademoiselle."

She smiled as I completed the sentence, and then got up.

"I should get going," she said. I still sat on my bed and looked up at her.

I nodded my head and replied, "Okay. Thanks for coming." She passed me a wide smile. I looked away and let out a wide yawn, covering my mouth with my right hand. Mini ma'am then said, "Hey, Nikita?"

I looked up at her as she stood next to my bed. "Yeah?"

She leaned down and whispered close to my face, "And remember: different, and proud." She patted my right cheek twice and said, "Take care."

I nodded my head and watched her walk out of my room. I looked down and smiled silently. I blinked once and looked up at the ceiling, speaking out so that it was only audible to me, "Different, and bloody proud."

eleven.

the next day...

"You're really obsessed with fictional characters, are you not?" Naaz asked as the two of us lay down on the green lush grass of my lawn, gazing up at the clear blue sky. I chuckled as I interlocked both my hands' fingers and rested them under my head. I sighed softly and answered, "Honestly, if I had a dollar for every time I felt more emotion for a fictional character than people in real life, I could pay for the psychiatric help I obviously need." She turned her head towards me and laughed, clapping her hands together like a seal. I looked at her and smiled, then shifted my gaze back at the sky. She stopped laughing after a moment and said, "You really are obsessed with fictional characters. Lovely." I smirked and yawned slightly. Naaz then asked, "So no real life crushes?" I looked at her and replied, sighing, "Not really, but now that you asked, my dad's best friend is pretty cute." Naaz shook her head and laughed sheepishly, I then said, "He's a doctor with a sense of humor, and he travels around the world! That is really, really cool. And he's adorable." I smiled as Naaz also smiled groggily and asked, "Can I ask a question?"

"Wasn't that a question itself?"

"Well…" She looked for a clever reply.

I chuckled. "Go ahead."

She sat up on the grass, her eyes sparkling as they lit up. She cleared her throat and asked, "Why did the chicken cross the road?"

I looked at her with a weird look pulled up on my face. I shook my head, stifling a chuckle. "Let's talk a little Sherlock-y here, shall we." I sat up, facing Naaz. I started to pluck a little of the green grass, almost by instinct. I, also like Naaz, cleared my throat, and then answered, "Because in his haste to leave home and go to see his mistress, the unfaithful farmer forgot to feed the chickens and carelessly left the gate to the coop open." I looked at Naaz and smiled slightly as she listened intently. I continued as I looked at my right hand plucking the grass from the ground, "One particularly clever fowl, conditioned to associate the sight of its owner with an expected feeling – basic psychology – saw him cross the road to his truck and followed him; a clever, but unfortunate move. The farmer neglected to check the rear view mirrors and ran the chicken over. I expect his wife will discover the affair since she finds the remnants of road-kill of the stupidly loyal fowl." I finished the sentence with a short sigh. I looked at Naaz as I chucked a fistful of the grass away. I laughed softly as her jaw dropped at my answer. She gulped as she pulled her jaw back into place.

"You know," I said, looking at Naaz. "We need to have new abbreviations for Facebook and Gmail and stuff."

"Mm, like what?" She asked as she yawned and snapped her right hand's fingers in front of her widely opened mouth.

"Like, ROFLTIRTIWMCMSISTC." I nodded my head, shutting my eyes as I folded my arms across my chest.

Naaz looked confused. "What?" She asked, totally zoned out.

I raised an eyebrow. "Rolling on the floor laughing till I realise that I won't marry Cillian Murphy so I start to cry."

She stifled a laugh and said, "That's going to take time to memorize, though." I threw my hands up into the air and replied, "Who cares? It's already going around in my head." She scratched the back of her head and shrugged her shoulders.

"It's kind of weird, isn't it?" I asked her as I gently fell back on the grass, looking up at the sky.

"What's weird?" said Naaz as she sat cross-legged on the grass.

I sighed and continued, "I'm pretty sure I'm going to be alone forever because Cillian is already married." Naaz rolled her eyes and gently nudged my leg with her foot.

I yawned and looked over at the gate as it creaked open. Lakshita came running in. Her eyes were sparkling with excitement as she skipped across the grass, a book in her hand.

"Nikita!" She exclaimed. Naaz and I looked up at her. I asked, "What's up?" She smiled and threw a thick novel down on my stomach, which then slipped and fell to the grass. I flinched slightly and sat up, picking up the book from the grassy ground. My eyes grew wide with excitement. I smiled widely and exclaimed, "Duuuuuude!" Lakshita folded her arms and nodded, "I know, riiiiiight?" I continued smiling and exclaimed again as I read the book's title, "Batman Begins: The Official Novelisation!" Lakshita flopped down on the ground next to me and Naaz.

Lakshita smiled widely. "I know! I got it in the mail today."

"Oh," My smile faded away. "I see you ordered it for yourself."

She looked at me and shook her head frantically, "No, no, no! I got this for you!"

My eyes lit up again. I looked at her and asked, "What, seriously?" She nodded her head, resting both her hands on the grass by her thighs. I opened up my arms and grabbed Lakshita, wrapping my arms around her tightly. I pulled away after a moment and smiled, saying, "This is awesome! You are awesome! Thank you so much."

I opened the book immediately and started flipping through the pages, my eyes filled with excitement and happiness. Lakshita smiled and then the conversation shifted to Lakshita and Naaz.

"Oh, hey, Naaz," said Lakshita. "Heh, sorry. I didn't notice you."

"Yes, with all the excitement in the air." Naaz said, not so excited.

"What, books don't interest you, I assume?" Lakshita asked.

"Not in the least." Naaz shook her head.

I rolled my eyes and looked up, sticking my tongue out at Naaz as the thought of her not loving books despised me. Naaz chuckled and looked at Lakshita as I continued eying the book's pages. Naaz then asked Lakshita, "Can you help me with something?" I fixed my eyes at a particular page and started reading it a little audibly. Lakshita scratched the inside of her right ear with her right hand's index finger, and said, "Anything, my friend."

Naaz bit the corner of her lips and shot a question through, "Is there a word for total screaming genius that sounds modest and a tiny bit sexy?"

Lakshita chuckled as she immediately recognized the line from her favourite episode of Doctor Who. As she was about to open her mouth to answer, I read out loud from the Batman Begins novel, my voice almost cracking with the excitement, "The name's Jonathan Crane."

Lakshita and Naaz looked at me, dazzled. Lakshita nodded her head and smiled, exclaiming, "Nice crossover, man!" Naaz nodded her head as well. I looked up at both of them, totally confused as to what they were saying. I narrowed my eyes and asked almost blankly, "Huh? Crossover what?"

Naaz gulped. "The thing you just did. The Jonathan Crane line."

I smiled slightly. "Oh, no. I just read out one of my most favourite lines from the Batman Begins novelisation."

Lakshita's jaw dropped. "What the—? Whoa." She looked up at the sky and continued, her Adam's apple throbbing as she gulped and addressed a fourth person, "You work wonders, my lord."

I shook my head and asked out of curiosity as I was totally zoned out of the conversation, "Tell me about this crossover thingie. What about it?" Naaz answered, "Well, I just picked up a random Doctor Who line and asked Lakshita if there was a word for total screaming genius that sounded modest and a tiny bit sexy."

Laskhita looked back at me and nodded quickly. "And that's when you read out the line, 'The name's Jonathan Crane.'"

I pouted my lower lip slightly and then bit my lower lip. I put myself forward into the conversation and said, "Well, Crane's a total screaming genius and..." I grinned slightly and continued, "...well, he's irresistibly sexy." I hopped up to my feet as I closed the book. I smiled down at them and whispered, "What a coincidence." I stretched my arms and yawned.

Lakshita looked up at me and said, "Damn. A brilliant coincidence." I looked at her and said, jumping up into the air slightly to stretch, "Speaking of..." I touched my feet on the ground and continued, "The Scarecrow is the best super-villain out there and no one can convince me otherwise." I turned around and started walking towards my house. I heard Naaz shout from behind, "We're not even contradicting that!"

I clicked my right hand's fingers into the air and shouted back, "You'd better not, for your sake."

Naaz and Lakshita started laughing.

twelve.

the next day...

I lay on my bed and stared up at the ceiling as my headphones covered my ears and my iPod played the movie Sunshine's OST.

Things hadn't improved between me and Ashwini since neither of the two of us had made an effort to text each other. I still sighed happily and closed my eyes, drowning myself in the calm music as I interlocked my fingers and put my hands under my head.

"Did you hear?" shouted Lakshita as she barged in through the door. I jumped up slightly and sat up immediately, removing my headphones from my ears. I put them around my neck, the music still playing, and looked up at her as I rubbed my eyes through my glasses.

"What?" I asked.

Lakshita folded her arms across her chest and said, "About Ashwini." I huffed slightly and scrunched, "What about Ashwini?"

"She's leaving for Chandigarh tonight."

I widened my eyes slightly and asked frantically, "Wait, what?" She nodded her head with her eyes shut. I looked down for a moment and then back at her, "How did you know?" Lakshita looked back at me and replied, "She called me up and asked me to come see her." I took a hard gulp and tried to hold back the emotion of having not been texted or called up by Ashwini. A weird silence fell. Lakshita and I stayed silent for a moment but then Lakshita broke the silence by saying, "I'm going there. You wanna come?" I looked up at her as I hugged my knees. I nodded once and then looked down, "Of course. I'd love to." Despite mine and Ashwini's differences, she was leaving, and I had to say goodbye. One last time.

Lakshita smiled. I got up from my bed and slipped into my slippers. I turned around on my toes and leaned down to press the pause button on my iPod. I led Lakshita out my bedroom's door and I walked downstairs with her. We walked out of my house and opened the metal gate. Lakshita stepped out first and I stepped out after her. I saw her father's silver Beamer standing there. I shoved my hands into my jeans' pockets and asked Lakshita, "I thought your father didn't like you and Dex being around his Beamer." Lakshita shook her head and walked towards the car and I followed in. She smiled slightly and replied, "He hates Dex anywhere near the car. As for me, I'm the responsible one." She smiled sweetly and leaned against the car's bonnet. I looked at her and grinned, "Well, unlock the doors. I've never rode in a BMW before." Lakshita smiled sheepishly and turned her neck towards the right so that she could see at the driver's seat through the black tinted windshield. I leaned slightly towards the left and saw someone sitting in. Quickly, the driver seat's window rolled down and Dhruv's head popped out.

"Hi," he said ever so charmingly. Over the past few days, I'd started to see Dhruv's other side – his real self. Him.

I chuckled and looked at Lakshita, smirked and said, "But your dad still doesn't let you drive a car, huh?" She took a deep breath and rolled her eyes and said in a very mocking tone, walking up to the car's backdoor "At least I don't have a crush on my dad's best friend." I scratched my right cheek and replied, "Naaz told you, wow."

"Oh, shut up," she said. I grinned widely and walked to the car's passenger seat. I opened the door and sat in.

"Wow," I said with a wide smile as I leaned back into the seat. "This is really comfortable." Dhruv nodded his head and turned the ignition on. He then backed the car out of our parking space and turned the car around and made way for Ashwini's house.

Dhruv then turned on the music system and the opening guitar riff to One Last Breath by Creed started playing through the speakers. I smiled as I heard the calm and peaceful music. Dhruv gripped the steering wheel a little tightly and smiled as he started singing along with the lyrics to One Last Breath by Creed, "Please come now, I think I'm falling. I'm holding on to all I think is safe." I smiled as he continued singing along with the rest of the song's lyrics and Lakshita and I joined in as well.

I smiled as we finished the song. The three of us started laughing. For just a single moment, it felt like all the happiness in the world was trapped in that silver sedan. It felt like nothing in the world could take any of it away. I didn't want the laughter to come to an end. That moment of pure happiness and ecstasy from singing a song all three of us knew.

Dhruv then cleared his throat after a moment as he turned the car into a narrow street. He said, "We should probably do a sleepover sometime."

"Let's do it," I smiled.

"That'd be fun!" exclaimed Lakshita as she leaned forward, bringing her head between Dex's and my headrest.

"And we could eat pizza and watch Katie Holmes' movies all night long!" said Dhruv, his voice ecstatic and his eyes sparkling. I shook my head in denial and protested politely, "Oh, no. It's either Cillian Murphy or Johnny Depp."

Dhruv narrowed his eyes and said, reeking of denial as well, "You don't get to make the decisions if we're having the sleepover at our place." I gritted my teeth together and clenched my jaw. I almost shouted in disgust, "Oh, balderdash and piffle."

"Katie!" shouted Dhruv.

"Cillian!" I shouted back.

"Ugh. Look at you two: quarrelling like a married couple!" shouted Lakshita from the behind.

Dhruv and I, both, turned our necks to face her. We shouted at her together, "SHUT UP!" She was taken aback slightly. She leaned back into her seat and mumbled under her breath, loud enough only for her to hear, "I'm dealing with kids here." Dhruv sighed and swallowed, his Adam's Apple loping up and down; his cheekbones as sharp as ever. One could cut themselves while slapping those perfect cheeks. I turned my head to the side and gazed out the window, looking at the leaves of trees as we passed them by, a subtle smile on my face.

Dhruv then said, his hand on the gearbox, "You know, Edison's last words were, 'It's beautiful there.' I don't know where there is, but I sure hope it's beautiful."

I turned my head back towards Dhruv and said politely, "It's right here." I smiled as I put my right hand over his left hand. He looked at my hand and then he looked at me, the ghost of a smile tugged at his lips.

thirteen.

Dhruv parked the car outside Ashwini's house and we got off as he pulled the key out of the keyhole. I shut the door behind me and looked over at Ashwini's house. I swallowed hard and thought of what I was going to talk to her about. I walked over to Dhruv's side which faced the main door to Ashwini's house. I leaned against the car's door and folded my arms, looking up at the house.

"Aren't you coming?" asked Lakshita as she walked towards the house. I shook my head and replied, "You guys go first. I'll go in when you come back." Dhruv tossed the car keys into the air and caught them back in his hand, and asked, "Sure about that?" I nodded my head and watched the two of them walk up to Ashwini's main door.

I sighed slightly as the door opened up and the two of them walked in, leaving me alone to my thoughts and the sound of dry leaves rustling on the ground. I walked over to the car's front and hopped up a little, sitting on the car's bonnet. I leaned back and put my hands under my head as I stared up at the sky. I sighed a little, both happily and sadly. I got lost in my own thoughts, questioning as to why Ashwini didn't tell me that she was leaving that night. Wondering why she didn't text or call me. The thought of that saddened me.

I shook my head and tried to divert my thoughts as I turned my neck slightly to the side and watched an old tree's shadows change shapes on the ground, forming figures. I chuckled slightly and hummed The Who's 'Behind Blue Eyes' to myself.

after a few minutes...

I heard the sound of footsteps walking towards the car. I opened my eyes and hopped off the bonnet as Lex and Dex walked back to the car. Dhruv pulled out the car keys and unlocked the car doors. I shoved my hands into my jeans' pockets and asked, "She holding up alright?" Lakshita nodded her head and replied, "Like she's going to be here tomorrow morning." I swallowed once and said, taking a deep breath, "Give me ten minutes, okay?" Dhruv smiled sweetly as he swung open the car's front door, and whispered lowly, "Take your time, please." I half smiled and tugged a lose end of my hair behind my right ear.

I walked up to Ashwini's house's front door and walked in, my hands in my jeans' pockets. I walked through the silenced lobby and knocked at Ashwini's room's closed door. "It's open," I heard her yell. I slowly opened the door and popped my head in.

"Hi," I said hesitantly. Ashwini looked up at me as she put her folded shirts into a red suitcase lying open on the bed. She smiled her usual smile and replied, "Nikita, come in, please." I walked in and shut the door behind me. I leaned against the door and sighed as I looked at all the stuff scattered on her bed. Books, clothes, toiletry and other supplies everywhere. She noticed me looking at her stuff. She chuckled sheepishly and said, "Well, it's quite a mess."

"The messiness is your organization." I smiled. I looked at her and pressed my lips together. I sighed and asked hesitantly, "How come you didn't tell me you were leaving for Chandigarh tonight?" She looked up at me as she folded a black top. She put it carefully into the suitcase and replied, "I just didn't want to go through the pain of saying goodbye to you."

"That's not worth believing." I rolled my eyes and looked away.

"I'm sorry."

I pursed my lips together and shook my head, still looking away as she tried to look into my eyes.

"You saved my life, Nikita," she said. "How do I bid goodbye to a life saver?"

I looked into her eyes and then looked down, shuffling my feet slightly, "I thought I was the one who was going to go away before you." I looked back up at her. "Seems it turned out different, huh? Plans took a different turn and I wasn't even aware."

She scratched her right temple and sighed. The two of us kept silent. I watched her as she shoved her slippers into a paper bag and put the paper bag into the suitcase, shoving it to the side. The suitcase was almost filled to the top as she brought the lid to the bag and zipped it up, putting a combination lock on. She flicked her hair to a side and looked up at me. She took a gulp of nothing and said, breaking the silence, "I'm really gonna miss you." I took a deep and shaky breath and replied, "I know, missy. I know." I half smiled and bit into my right cheek, looking straight into her eyes.

"But," she said, squeezing her eyes shut. "School."

I blinked and replied jokingly, "You'll get busy with your own life. +1 isn't going to be easy for either of the two of us. You'll barely have time for yourself, let alone have time for your friends."

She kept silent.

I sighed deeply and continued, "We grow up, Ashwini. Forget people of the past. Get over shit. Deal with problems. We barely get time for ourselves. It's alright. It's this screwed-up thing called life. Happens to everyone." I shrugged my shoulders. "God, I should write a self-help book."

Ashwini shook her head quickly and shouted, opening her eyes. Her eyes welled up as she shouted, "Whatever! I don't like change! I'm hating this fact!" She pulled up a long face as she finished her sentence. I blinked a few times before replying politely, "You'll get used to me not being around and vice-versa. Maybe a haunted figure will linger about." I smiled my usual crooked smile as I completed my sentence and looked up at her. She took a deep breath and said, "Oh, please. Just shut up." I nodded my head with a slight shrug of my shoulders. She wiped off her tears and shook her head, pretending like tears never emerged from her eyes.

I smiled slightly and said, "I should get going now." She looked up at me and took a step forward as she nodded her head.

"You take care of yourself and all the very best," I said as I reached my hand forward for a handshake.

With little distance between us, she reached her hand forward as well to take a hold of my hand. She grabbed my hand and quickly pulled me to her. I blinked as she wrapped her arms around me and buried her face in my right shoulder. I hugged her back, rubbing her back lovingly, trying to comfort her.

I whispered lowly into her ear, "It's okay. I'm okay. You're okay. We're okay." She nodded her head and sobbed into my shoulder. I continued to hold her close for a few moments.

She then pulled away after a few moments, swallowing hard as she wiped off her tears using the palms of both her hands. She sighed and looked at me as I shoved my hands into my jeans' pockets. I took a step backwards and whispered a question, "What am I, Ashwini?"

She blinked and asked back, "Is that supposed to be a trick question?" I shrugged my shoulders.

"You're human. A little less than others, but you're human," she said with a sigh.

"Nikita Achanta," I whispered as our gaze met. "The angel with the devil's smug grin and wings. Your beautiful lie. Your best friend."

We exchanged smiles for one last time as I adjusted my glasses and opened the door to walk out of the room. I walked out of her room, my smile fading away as I felt that horrible lump in the back of my throat. I felt my eyes welling up. I shook my head and sucked the emotion and sentiment back. I sighed deeply but smiled slightly as I walked out of Ashwini's house, perhaps for the last time.

fourteen.

two days later...

I sighed as I sat on top of a small hill just outside of town. A hill that looked down upon the entire city. I sat cross legged on the grass, my bike standing next to me as I looked at the red sun almost ready to set. I sat all by myself. Just the sound of birds chirping as they made their way home, leaves rustling, the wind blowing through my hair.

"Spending some quality time with yourself, yes?" I heard Dhruv say.

I turned my head upside down to take a look up at him as he approached me. I chuckled and looked ahead. A question escaped my lips, "How did you know I'd be here?" He came and sat down on the grass next to me. He hugged his knees and looked at the setting sun. He replied, "I knew you'd be here. You're here whenever you're upset or just feeling lonely." I looked at him and nudged his arm playfully with my elbow. I smiled softly and looked at him, "Or to think." He nodded his head and looked back at me, smiling, "Uh huh." We looked into each other's eyes for a moment. I then snapped out of it and looked forward, chuckling to myself.

I sighed softly and said out of the blue, "It's strange, you know." Dhruv looked at me and asked, "What is?" I took a deep breath and continued, "This feeling about caring about someone. Feeling a little detached when they leave. It just feels weird." He scooted closer to me as he listened intently. He leaned his head towards me slightly and whispered, "It's a part of being human. I care about you." I looked up at him and into his eyes, a weird spark in his eyes. I bit my lower lip and asked, "Why?" He blinked and pulled away almost instantly.

"What kind of a question is that?" he asked.

"You know I'm only going to end up hurting you in the end."

"It hurts because it matters."

I looked deeper into his eyes and swallowed hard, my Adam's Apple moving up and down quickly. He slowly wrapped an arm around my shoulder and pulled himself closer to me, saying, "And anyway, it would be a privilege to have my heart broken by you, Hazel Grace." I felt the warmth of his arm against my shoulder. I hesitated a little but then shook my head as I moved myself closer to him, no space in between us as I leaned my head against his shoulder. I laughed a little as he referred to me as John Green's Fault In Our Stars' protagonist Hazel Grace. I smiled and snuggled close to him, wrapping both my arms around his torso. He gently played with a lock of my hair, twirling it in between his fingers.

"Look at me," I said to him.

He looked at me, no expressions on his face or in his eyes. I quickly took a hold of his white shirt's collar and pulled him closer to me with a jerk, pressing my forehead against his as I looked deeply into his eyes. I breathed a little heavily. I placed my free hand on his chest, near his heart. I smiled slightly as I felt his heart race. He looked back into my eyes and bit his lower lip. I took a deep breath and then finally leaned forward, pressing my lips gently to his. I squeezed my eyes shut, wrapping both my arms around his neck. He blinked as I pulled him into a kiss. He quickly wrapped his arms around my waist and pulled me closer to him as he closed his eyes as well. I smiled against his lips and worked mine with his. He bit my lower lip playfully and I placed my hands gently on his neck. I opened my eyes slowly and then pulled away, realising what I'd done. I pulled my hands away as well and blinked. He looked at me and pulled himself and his arms away.

He smiled sheepishly. I laughed lightly and we looked at each other.

"Let's not talk about this ever again," I said, nodding.

He nodded quickly and replied, "Good idea." I chuckled and hugged my knees, looking at the weather horizon and the sun slowly disappeared, departing from the clear orange sky. I then looked at Dhruv and said, raising up a clenched fist at him, "Fist bump?" He smiled and gently bumped his fist against mine.

"Hey, listen," I said.

He looked at me as the two of us got up on our feet. He dusted the dirt off of his FCB shorts. "Yes?"

"Don't try to get into my head – you will only find a mess," I took a gulp of nothing, my eyes inanimate.

The two of us looked at each other for a while in utter silence. Dhruv broke the silence as he put on his classic crooked smile and said, his tone soft and tender, "I'm ready to sort it out."

I finally gave in to a smile and the two of us laughed slightly. I sighed and said, "There's this thing Alan Shore says to Denny Crane in one of the Boston Legal episodes, and I guess it applies to the both of us."

Curiosity sparked in his eyes. "And which is?"

I cleared my throat and began to quote Alan Shore, "People walk around calling everyone their best friend. The term doesn't have any real meaning anymore. Mere acquaintances are lavished with hugs and kisses upon a second or, at most, third meeting. Birthday cards get passed around offices so everybody can scribble a snippet of sentimentality for a colleague they barely met. Everyone just loves everyone. As a result when you tell somebody you love them today. It isn't much heard. I love you, Denny, you are my best friend. I couldn't imagine going through life without you as my best friend." I took a deep breath as Dhruv looked at me, dumbfound. I coughed a little and continued, "Alan and Denny end up getting married, don't worry, I'm not friendzoning you." Dhruv laughed a little and replied, "Yeah, I know. But it's beautiful. Thank you, Nikita."

I smiled and he smiled as well as the two of us looked at each other.

He was so beautiful. So perfect. He could easily be the Augustus Waters to my Hazel Grace and I wouldn't mind.

fifteen.

the next day...

Lakshita and I sat on a local park's bench. I pressed my right hand to my forehead as it throbbed. I squeezed my eyes shut in anger and frustration as I heard the sound of two babies crying. It was cacophony to my ears and their mother seemed to do nothing about it. I looked over at Lakshita as she continued reading my copy of John Green's The Fault in Our Stars.

I nudged her right arm with my left elbow and said, "This is getting annoying." She nodded her head but kept her concentration and eyes on the book. She replied, "I can't do anything about it, Nikita." I sighed deeply and asked, "Can we please leave?"

She shook her head and looked at me. Then she looked around and at the crying babies. She pulled up a sympathetic look and her puppy eyes. She moaned softly and said, "Aw, the baby's crying. Oh, the poor sweet thing. I hope he doesn't cry further. He'll be okay."

I gritted my teeth and squeezed my eyes shut. I then let out a groan and almost yelled over the whines in the air, "Shut the hell up! Someone take it back home! Why do people keep having these things?!"

Lakshita's jaw dropped. She looked at me and took a gulp as all the eyes around us turned towards me. I rolled my eyes and got up from the bench. My head started aching even more. I stomped my right foot on the ground and walked away without a further word to Lakshita, leaving her alone to digest the embarrassment.

Soon after, as I was walking on the interior pavement, Lakshita caught up with me. She held the closed novel in her right hand, pressed up against her thigh. She started taking heavy steps to draw my attention towards her. I huffed and looked at her.

"Now what?" I asked.

"Nikita," she took a deep breath. "What are you?"

"Is that supposed to be a trick question?"

She shrugged her shoulders. I chuckled and thought of a humorous answer but failed to come up with one. So I flicked my hair away from my forehead and answered, "Well, my dad's a doctor. My mum's a doctor. And my brother, too, is a doctor." She looked back at me and watched me curiously. I smiled and continued, "Fangirl. I'm a fangirl, through and through."

She huffed lightly and rolled her eyes playfully. "A little more specific?"

I stifled a laugh. "Well, I am just a fun-filled little lollipop triple dipped in psycho."

She burst out into a fit of giggles. I smiled and shoved my hands into my Barcelona FC shorts, shuffling my feet as we walked on the pavement. I sighed and started humming the tune to Alien Ant Farm's cover of Michael Jackson's Smooth Criminal. "But mama, I'm in love with a criminal."

Lakshita looked at me with a deranged look and asked, "Nikita, what?"

I rolled my eyes and replied, "As in, Jim Moriarty, dude."

"Ah, the Napoleon of Crime," she said, gazing dramatically into the distance. I nudged her arm playfully and replied, "Brilliant man."

"He had a sticky end."

"Can't say Moriarty didn't."

"I'm sorry he died," she said sympathetically. Lakshita looked down and kicked a small rock out of her way. I shrugged my shoulders and replied in a Moriarty-y tone, "That's what people do."

The two of us looked at each other, serious for one moment. But just one. Then we started laughing, unable to control ourselves. I shook my head, trying to contain my laughter.

"I'm serious! You need to stop making me laugh in situations like these," I said with a nod. She shrugged her shoulders, still laughing. I shook my head and looked away, a smile tugged at my lips.

I stopped laughing as I took a deep breath and saw a familiar face. There stood Mini ma'am with her soon-to-be-thirteen daughter, Sarah, near the park's pavement bound by a railing, which looked down upon a line of fountains. I gave Lakshita's arm a nudge and turned my head towards her.

"I spy with my little eye a familiar face," I said. She looked at me and then peeked past me. She smiled softly and replied, "Two familiar faces, to be exact."

I rolled my eyes playfully and lightly smacked her across the face with my right hand.

"Come on," I smiled and Lakshita and I approached the two of them. Lakshita matched her feet with mine. Sarah soon turned her head towards the two of us. I saw a smile sneak up on her face.

"Nikita Achanta, the person who shows up almost everywhere my mum and I go," she said, mocking me. I shoved my hands into my shorts' pockets and played along as I stood steps away from her. I sighed a little and replied like Benedick from Shakespeare's Much Ado About Nothing, "Nay, nay, mock not! Lakshita and I came here before you."

She folded her arms across her chest and said, "Like I caaaaare."

I gritted my teeth. "Screw—"

"Nikita," said Lakshita as she wrapped her left hand around my right wrist. "No swearing in public places, remember?" I shook my hand, forcing her hand away.

"Nikita," I heard Mini ma'am say. She turned towards us and smiled. "What a coincidence."

"Coincidence indeed," interrupted Sarah with annoyance in her voice. I exhaled loudly and asked, "Kid, what is your problem with me?" She shook her head and replied, "Nothing, really. I'm just not a big fan of yours, to be honest." I nodded my head and pulled my hands out of my pockets.

"Fair enough," I grinned, playing along. "Here, here, Lakshita," I grabbed Sarah's right wrist and pulled her towards Lakshita. "Go on. Play along, the two of you." I smiled my crooked smile and playfully waved at

Lakshita. Lakshita rolled her eyes and shifted her gaze to Sarah, indulging her in a conversation.

I turned to Mini ma'am and bowed my head slightly.

"Always charming to meet you," I said with a smile. She chuckled and replied, "I see you and Sarah still don't get along well." I nodded my head and said, "And we never will. But," Mini ma'am looked at me. I whispered lowly, "That won't stop me from coming to her birthday party." I opened up my arms and continued, "Free food!"

"You do love food." She laughed softly and nodded once.

"Especially when it's free." I winked at her.

She smiled and said, her voice low, "You're so cute."

I narrowed my eyes slightly and shook my head twice. "Don't call me cute."

"But you are cute."

I chuckled softly and looked away, slightly embarrassed. I then looked back at her and whispered softly, quoting Jim Moriarty, "I will burn the heart out of you." I grinned slightly, shoving my hands back into my pockets.

"Yeah, yeah," she rolled her eyes. I scratched my right cheek with my index finger and yawned slightly.

"Nikita?" she asked as I gazed up at the blue sky, leaning against the railing with my arms crossed across my chest. I looked at her and she looked back at me, placing an arm on the railing. "Thank you," she said softly. I tilted my head to the right and asked, confused, "What for?" She bit her lower lip, nipping at it lightly. She sighed softly and answered, "For

227

everything." I shrugged my shoulders in disapproval and said, shifting my gaze back to the water shooting up into the sky from the fountains.

I took a deep breath. "Remember, almost a year back, when I stood second in that interschool debate I was so hesitant to participate in and I thanked you for giving me the courage, and then you said that I didn't have to thank you for anything at all?"

She looked at me and nodded her head, not saying anything else.

I smiled and continued, turning my head to her, "If you say that I can't thank you for the slightest of things, then that gives you no right to thank me."

A smile snuck onto her face and spread across her lips. She looked down and then at the fountains. She nodded her head and said, "Fair enough." I smiled softly to myself and sighed happily, tapping my left hand's fingers lightly on my right forearm.

Mini ma'am then looked at me and said, "You're a catastrophe, you know that?" I sighed deeply and looked back at her. Rolling my eyes and shifting my gaze back to the fountains, I said nothing.

"A beautiful catastrophe," she continued as she pursed her lips together.

I looked over at her almost as soon as she completed her sentence. I smiled to myself, at a loss of words, not knowing what to say. She left me speechless with three little words and I said nothing but gave her a single nod.

part four.

wordsmith.

unconditional love.

My mother says that a mother has unconditional love towards her children. "So if I break a vase or something, mum's not going to be mad at me?" – popped into my head. The second thing was – "Hmm, so if I don't get over 80 in my math exam, mum won't ground me?"

Unconditional love is love without any limitations. See, we teens cannot have unconditional love towards anyone. I mean, have you seen my generation? At times I wonder how I ended up here. Anyway, so this 'unconditional love' is something that every mum has towards their child. I'm a good student – obedient, hardworking, but sometimes a little stubborn when it comes to solving math problems. My mum loves me still. No matter how many times I mess up, make her pull her hair, demand too much, ask for Batman figures or even make her unhappy, she doesn't actually become mad at me and throw a vase at me or ask me to leave the house. No matter how many times I talk to her rudely because I'm mad at someone, she actually doesn't leave me. Even at the end of the day, mum is the only person who's still there for me – standing there in that shining white light, arms wide open, smiling. And even if a child isn't bloody brilliant at everything, his mother still loves him. Always has from the first day he could hold her finger and smile silently, to this day when he's walking.

Unconditional love towards her child is what a mother offers. I don't get it why people say that they have unconditional love towards their boyfriend or friends. I mean, how can you? You can't. They mess things up, you get mad. But if you mess up something in front of your mum, she'll snap a little and then, she'll chuckle a little. Why? Because she's a mother and her love knows no limit.

how does love work?

Honestly, I thought I was going to spend a night going without sleep, getting high on three cups of coffee, racking my brain off trying to write an essay on Julius Caesar. And that might have been easier, because I'm sitting here right now, thinking, "How does love actually work?" No, I'm not amused and I don't even know how this article's going to turn out.

Love. Weird word, isn't it? One word that can completely ruin the human brain's working, just because of one person. Well, that's how the human brain works. Love is something that makes you so vulnerable. It opens your chest and opens your heart and it means that someone can get inside you and mess you up. You build up all these defences. You build up this whole armour, for years, so no one can hurt you, then one stupid person, no different from any other stupid person, wanders into your stupid and pathetic, meaningless life. You give them a piece of you. They don't ask for it. They do something dumb one day, like smile at you, and then your life isn't your own anymore. Love takes hostages. It gets inside you. It eats you out and leaves you crying in the darkness, so a simple phrase like 'maybe we should just be friends' turns into a glass splinter working its way into your heart. It hurts. Not just in the mind. It's a soul hurt, a body hurt, a real gets-inside-you-and-rips-you-apart pain.

Sorry, that's just one of my favourite quotations and I just thought of putting it in here because it seemed appropriate. So basically, love is this weird feeling inside of you which gives you butterflies in your stomach when you see that special person. I get butterflies every time I see Johnny Depp, which kind of explains it.

Let's see how this happens, according to me:

- One person walks into your life.
- They smile at you. That melts your heart.
- You can't take it.
- You start to stalk them.
- Okay, scratch the stalking part.
- You start to like them.
- Then, one crazy day, your heart goes all, "You see him? Yeah, you're in love with him."
- Your heart overpowers your brain, freezing all your five senses.
- I know, how screwed up is that?
- Then suddenly, your heart decides to get attached.
- You talk to them, you smile with them, and you laugh with them, till you reach a point of no return.
- Then, one crazy day, this one special person decides to stop speaking to you.

- No reason at all.
- That breaks your heart.
- You get no sleep at night.
- You put depressing Facebook statuses just to get some sympathy or attention or whatever.
- Attention-seeking brat.
- You get upset over the littlest of things.
- You fight with your friends.
- You get angry at everyone.
- You munch on tons of chocolate every day, hoping it would cool it off. (Honestly, I think it's the dementors.)
- You curse yourself for everything.
- And that one special person doesn't give two shits about you.
- Then you suddenly decide to move on, but it's not that easy.
- Then, you suddenly wake up one dreadful morning, feeling so mad, and you say to yourself, "No, screw this. I don't give a damn about you anymore."
- So your heart starts hating everyone of that gender.
- Happy ever after.

See what I'm getting at? To be very honest, the human brain is a pretty messed up thing. It can't do anything once your heart takes over. And love is what ruins everything. I'm still looking for answers as to why isn't everyone like me? Hate everyone! Problem solved.

Why, in every movie, does the protagonist always make stupid decisions? Well, look! There's a girl involved. It's "love". Craziness. See? This is exactly why I always side with the villains, because they don't care about anyone. They hate everyone. And I hate everyone. This means I'm a super-villain. Hah.

Love is one disease that messes everything in the system. It screws everything up. It takes over your heart which, eventually, takes over your brain. Love has its own pros and cons. As a hater of everything, I can only look at its cons. I mean, loving one's family is a different thing. Loving friends is alright. But "falling in love" with someone? Now that's something I just don't get. Maybe it's just me. But love has the nasty habit of disappearing overnight.

But you can fall in love like me. I fell in love with my Harry Potter books. It was love at first sight. I've been in love with Cillian Murphy since forever now. I love him so much, it hurts.

So for all that works, and since the human brain is so screwed up, you can figure out why I'm in love with Cillian Murphy and Johnny Depp. That will be all.

confessions.

Confession #1.

I don't feel like a friend to most people. I feel more like an option or someone they can run to when they need anything. Which is why I spend most of my weekends at home, listening to my iPod all day long. And plus, I hate attachment and feelings. Their outcome is nothing but pain and misery.

Confession #2.

I'm an atheist. THIS IS NO WAY INTENDED TO OFFEND ANYONE. What I think is that people came up with the concept of god because they couldn't define certain things, like, "Why do the stars shine?" or some shit. If there's a god I do worship, it's Cillian Murphy. Okay, that man is a sex god. 'Nuff said.

Confession #3.

I think my feelings for my bed are much MUCH stronger than they are for humans. Therefore, I'm in a relationship with my bed. Problem?

Confession #4.

I grew into a fan of Cillian Murphy about three years back when I saw Red Eye. Something about him just attracted me like crazy. His blue eyes attracted me like a freaking magnet. His blue eyes. His cheekbones. His hair. His lips. His perfect nose. His face. HIS ENTIRE BODY. I don't even know, HIM. I've never been so obsessed with a celebrity before and now it's like my life revolves around Cillian. Whenever he embarrasses himself in an interview or behind-the-scenes videos, I feel like a part of myself just embarrassed itself. A smile quickly sneaks onto my face whenever I look at a photo of Cillian or watch his interviews. I feel so attached to him and so in love with him even if he doesn't know of my existence. And he dies in almost every movie of his. And when he does, I feel a part of me dying and I just can't stop the tears from streaming down my face. I just feel so dead inside. Anyway, point is that Cilly is the only celebrity I've been so in love with. I swear, if I get to meet him one day, I'll faint, thanks to his deep blue eyes. And yeah, that's about it. I love him.

Confession #5.

Cillian Murphy, Johnny Depp, Stana Katic and Liv Tyler are the ones who completely changed my worldview. It's like I feel stronger inside reading their articles and watching their interviews or going through some of their quotes. These four inspire me BIGLY. I can never thank them enough for all they've given to me.

Confession #6.

Poets of the Fall is THE band that saved my life. Don't know them? Look them up. You'll love them. I do. Next to Cillian Murphy and pizza, I love POTF the most.

Confession #7.

The Beatles are my favorite band. I know they broke up but I still feel so close to them. Their music is amazing and they still live on in a million hearts. They're legendary and no one, according to me, will ever be able to replace them.

Confession #8.

I love people on the internet WAY more than I love people around me. So there.

Confession #9.

I WANNA BE IRISH IN MY NEXT LIFE.

Confession #10.

I don't think I ever want to "get into a relationship". Ugh. No. Too many responsibilities. Plus, like I said, I fucking hate feelings and attachment. I'm better off with my books, guitar, and music.

Confession #11.

The Harry Potter books and movies completely altered my life. All that I am today is mostly because of HP. I've read all the HP books at least thrice and I still can't get enough of it. I still cry at certain moments. I still cry whenever a death occurs in the books. I'm just so in love with all my HP books. I can never thank JKR enough for giving me the best childhood any kid could ever ask for.

Confession #12.

If The Beatles or Pink Floyd are your favorite band, we can be best friends.

Confession #13.

I'm mentally married to Cillian Murphy. Deal with it.

Confession #14.

I'm a hardcore grammar Nazi. I just, I don't know, can't stand "text lingo". It gets on my nerves and irritates me like hell.

Confession #15.

I hate it when people text me too many red heart emoticons. Red hearts make me cringe.

Confession #16. Last one.

I can laugh and joke and smile and pretend as if nothing's wrong and that I lead a perfectly happy teenage during the day, but sometimes, when I'm alone at night, I forget how to feel. And that sucks. Trust me, you never want experience that. It's like you're dead inside. And that's not nice.

what music means to me.

I've been attracted by the sound of music since I was a little child. From silly nursery rhymes that made no sense at all to theme songs of my favourite cartoon shows, music was always the main attraction for me. As I grew up, I was introduced to various genres of music but Hindi music from films never attracted me. It always made me sad because all the songs in Hindi movies were love-songs and made no sense to me. When I turned eight, my father introduced me to Pink Floyd. The first English song that I ever listened to was 'Another Brick in the Wall' by Pink Floyd, and that was the song that had such an impact on me because of the lyrics and the music and I was immediately attracted to English music.

If there's one thing that means a lot to me, other than my family, it's music. Music has completely changed my outlook of and the way I look at this world. It's made me a better person. Bands like The Beatles, Pink Floyd, Linkin Park, Poets of the Fall, Green Day and Paramore have gotten me through so many things. There are songs I can relate to in certain situations and songs that make me feel better than most humans. Something that my family and so-called friends fail to do, music does. Music has made me grow more confident. As I'm getting older, my fondness for music is growing. When kids in my class say that they 'love music', they mean that they listen to music for about two to three hours a day and that's it. No, music is something more. Music, to me, is much more than, as most of my friends say, 'noise and random guitar'. I don't believe that anybody feels the way I do towards music. I listen to music for almost the entire day. Whenever I'm doing my homework, Pink Floyd or The Beatles are playing on my laptop because they give me a boost. Something I cannot fathom into words. Some songs are so deep that they hit you immediately, which is why I don't like to listen to the autotuned songs and singers these days like Justin Bieber and Lady Gaga.

Some of the greatest songwriters of all time, like John Lennon, have been through the challenges that every other teenager faces but they came out to be something more than just humans. They are an entirely different species. They are legends that will never fade away. And their stories have inspired me as well. Whenever I'm down or feel like an underachiever, listening to songs like 'Working Class Hero' cheers me up instantly. Songs like these give me strength and inspire me to be something bigger. And that's where my positivity and optimism comes from.

> Music, along with books, is my escape from the hustle bustle of this world. Listening to the voices of my favourite bands and singers brings peace to my mind.

Music, to me, is like meditation. Whenever I have my headphones on or am listening to music on my laptop, I feel at peace with myself no matter how bad my day went.

Music has brought about my creativity that no human ever could have. Grade seventh, I started writing poetry and articles because that's what many songs inspired me to do. To follow one's dreams.

Music has definitely made me a better human being than I was before. All that I am at the age of sixteen today is mainly because of my love and dedication towards music.

It's a stress buster for me because whenever I'm down or heavily stressed, which I am a lot, music lifts my spirits higher and reenergizes me, giving me strength to march fourth.

Music has helped me understand about the many aspects of life like hatred, love, care, materialism and expectation, something the formal education and the environment in which I grew up failed to do miserably.

Music means so much to me. More than most humans, to be honest.

Aut viam inveniam aut faciam

~I shall either find a way or make one~